THE BLIND SIDE

D1002661

THE
BLIND
SIDE

Francis Clifford

Academy
Chicago
Publishers

Published in 1985 by

Academy Chicago Publishers
425 N. Michigan Ave.
Chicago, Illinois 60611

Copyright © 1971 by
J.B. Thompson

Printed and bound in the U.S.A.

Library of Congress Cataloging-in-Publication Data
Clifford, Francis.
    The blind side.

    Reprint. Originally published: New York : Pocket Books, 1971.
    I. Title.
PR6070.H66B5   1985   823'.914   85-18591
ISBN 0-89733-170-2

For
Joanne and Charles

BOOK ONE

CHAPTER ONE

1

War or no war, the rains came no later than May. In living memory it had always been so, and even at the best of times the rains meant the start of the famine season. But the best of times belonged to the past; two years' fighting had insured that. And now, without warning, the vital relief column had ceased to deliver. All at once mere subsistence was no longer the issue. Before June was halfway through they were starving to death in the outlying villages, and in Abaguma itself the signs of what was in store were there for all to see.

The old were the first to die; mostly they seemed to wither a little more, shrivel a little more, then quietly perish in their huts. The diseased and the very young lingered longer because of self-sacrifice by their families or because they had priority in the mission hospital and the makeshift refugee camp nearby. But they could not last indefinitely; without adequate protein, vitamins and drugs their condition was irreversible. Mercy alone was not enough. Rations were halved and halved again, but no trucks arrived. The marks of ravaging hunger began to show even among the able-bodied—piebald patches on flaking skin, fluid-swollen bellies, leaking pustules disfiguring skeletal limbs, lethargic eyes sodden with pain. Once starvation got a hold on the weak the decline was swift. And who, by the start of the third year, was strong?

Some squatted around the hospital compound in the

hope of admittance when death made room inside, others sprawled in self-abandonment about the open spaces of the town; few walked with purpose or destination except for the burial squads. Flies and bugs apart, almost the only other living things to move were the vultures planing obscenely in to hunch on roofs and trees. No livestock remained: even the bush rat had become a luxury. But still nothing came up the swampy, tortuous road from the south and the small town's reserves of stockfish and dried milk rapidly dwindled away.

Sometimes, as the day sweltered to an end, a concerted chanting moaned from the refugee camp; sometimes gunfire trembled in from the blurred distances as if to remind everyone why they suffered. But for much of the day and night Abaguma was as silent as the grave and the smell of the hot drenched earth was everywhere, like that of death itself.

2

June ended, and Richard Lawrence knew it was futile to delay any longer. On the first Friday of July he finished saying mass in the tiny, open-sided church and immediately made his way to the hospital. There was no one to speak to when mass ended: the rows of benches rooted under the thatch were empty. Despair had gone deep. He walked wearily across the clearing separating the church from the hospital, and those who were gathered there lifted fevered eyes to him in appeal or raised skinny, cupped hands saying "fa-da . . . fa-da" as he passed.

The hospital consisted of three long, single-story buildings with a few huts scattered about the fenced perimeter. Richard pushed through the gate into the compound: again cracked voices pleaded with him, asking the impossible, but he had reached a stage where pity merely numbed. Slumped beside the door of the main building an old goitered woman was having her hair deloused by an emaciated young girl who gazed at him mindlessly. The building was of wood, with a tin roof, the floor raised to escape ants. Richard mounted the creaking steps and went inside, the door flapping behind him as he looked for Sister Marie along the length of the crowded mattress-strewn interior. She was at the far end and he made his way toward her, stepping carefully between the litter of recumbent bodies.

"D'you know where Albert is?"

"He was here minutes ago." Her pale face was drawn, the eyes dark-ringed. For years she and Sister Assumpta had run this place with Dr. Okawe's help, anointing for craw-craw, injecting for yaws, prescribing for malaria, and they ran it still although their resources were overwhelmed and their strength at breaking point. Richard had never failed to marvel, not even now when desperation gripped him.

"I'm going south, sister. Something has to be done. We can't keep on like this."

"Where are you going?" He might have been about to desert.

"Uziama." Thirty to thirty-five miles. "They've opened an airstrip there. Supplies are getting in. I heard on the radio last night."

A huddled figure cried out, like a dog choking. "Coming," Sister Marie called, her soft Kerry brogue suddenly more marked.

"We're entitled to a share." Richard followed her to the side of a twitching, unnaturally swollen youth. "Whoever's in charge at Uziama needs to be reminded of our existence—and quickly, before it's too late."

For a month all the lines had been down. Public services were nonexistent. The urgent letters dispatched by messenger to diocesan and civil headquarters had never been answered, perhaps never delivered; the messengers themselves had not returned. Troops straggled sporadically through the district, but they were no better informed than anyone else. The radio was the only remaining link with what went on beyond the jungle-clad horizon, yet mostly it dealt in threats and promises rather than facts: Uziama was an exception. Abaguma had always been a backwater. Now it had been forgotten, forgotten or cut off—which didn't matter. And

3

Sister Marie knew it; in their hearts all four of them knew it.

"When will you go?"

"Today," Richard said. "At once. If I'd had any sense I should have gone before June was out. But I have to see Albert first." He paused. For a moment he thought she was about to argue with him, but he was mistaken. A slight nod and he was dismissed, as if she needed to conserve every scrap of strength for others.

"I'll be back as soon as I possibly can."

Richard found Dr. Okawe in the third hut; Sister Assumpta was with him. There was a time when she had always been gay and quick to laugh, but the past few weeks had taken their toll. The brightness had gone, the young brown eyes dulled; she looked about as sick as those she tended. Grim-faced, Albert Okawe glanced up from a woman in fevered labor, his glistening black skin taut across the bones.

"Six more died during the night," he said flatly.

"I wasn't sent for."

"None of them was yours."

Richard shrugged. Numbers had ceased to mean anything. He had buried over eighty Catholics during June alone and for every man, woman and child who received the last rites there were at least two who had died groaning to their age-old pagan gods. And every death was a waste, an affront, a scandal.

"I want a word with you, Albert."

Together they picked a path to the curtained lobby and its rickety desk littered with crudely kept medical records. The doctor nodded, thick lips pursed, when Richard told him of his intention.

"You have nothing to lose. In my opinion, we've been left to rot."

"The rivers may have become impassable." An effort was required to be charitable; bitterness was easier. "Anyway, I'll soon know the answer."

"How early are you leaving?"

"Within the hour. Give me a list of what you're most short of, will you?"

Richard gazed briefly along the packed floor: even the

4

spaces between the beds were filled. He would be needed again before the day was done; yet if Abaguma were left to fend for itself any longer, those who survived would soon be going to their shallow graves by the hundred.

"Good luck, father," Albert said impassively. "I'll have a list ready in time."

<h1 style="text-align:center">3</h1>

The refugees who had flocked into Abaguma from the battlefronts occupied an area of level ground to the west of the town. There were already nearly a thousand of them, mostly women and children. The camp had no precise boundaries except for a stream along its northern side, but the refugees did not spread themselves. They huddled close, as if for safety, drawn together into forlorn groups to share what protection they could collectively muster against the damp and the rain.

Increasingly the stench of ordure mingled with the acrid combination of wood smoke and sopping vegetation. It filled Richard's nostrils as he drove past in the Land Rover. The camp's needs required no clarification, but the doctor's list in his pocket was formidable. "You're expecting miracles," he'd said almost in protest as he turned to leave, and Albert had replied: "Half a miracle will do. Anything will be better than nothing."

The Land Rover was the only working vehicle remaining in Abaguma and the last of the town's petrol was in its tank. To begin with, the dirt road ran parallel with the stream. Beyond the stream the twin peaks of Broken Tooth Mountain showed through the hazed air. Here, as elsewhere, Richard's feeling was that the jungle would win in the end; people were only tenants. He drove carefully, nursing the Land Rover through the worst of the ruts. To his knowledge, nothing except the odd bicycle had passed this way for the best part of a month; the ruts belonged to the time when traffic had flowed with comparative freedom between Abaguma and the provincial capital. Now flies swarmed in an iridescent veneer on a putrid carcass and the greasy, skinless road turned and twisted deeper into the green gloom.

Richard had left his home by the church at just on nine. At half past it began to rain again, spattering sullenly on the canvas top. Soon it was like driving on a skid-patch. Progress was arduous and desperately slow. It was over an hour before he reached the junction of stream and river, the first of the big rivers walled by huge trees. As expected, no one was in attendance at the ferry point; the people who until recently had occupied the village on the far bank were among the earliest to converge on Abaguma. Richard ran the Land Rover onto the heavy raft and hauled himself across by the heavy creeper ropes. The river was sluggish, the current negligible, and he moved the raft without much difficulty.

Others, he told himself, could surely have done the same. Anyone with determination could have brought half a dozen laden trucks across from the south. It was difficult to withhold judgment. Abaguma lay in the back of beyond and knew something about hardship and isolation when the crops failed or the rivers flooded, yet the sense of abandonment smoldered in Richard's mind. Perhaps, when he reached Lazaru, Tim O'Leary could enlighten him. It was surprising not to have had word from Tim. Were chaos and disruption so complete? Until the last few days Biafra Radio had spoken interminably of military success and ultimate victory.

Beyond the empty village the trees fell away and there were stretches of elephant grass to either side, sometimes reaching as far as the rain-smudged base of the hills. For another few hard-fought miles the longish vistas remained; then the scrub closed in again, the lush scrub and the dripping trees, and the Land Rover's wheels floundered deeper in marshlike mud. Often it was all Richard could do to maintain direction or avoid becoming totally bogged down. By noon he had covered no more than a dozen miles, and he was repeatedly being made aware that starvation was not confined to Abaguma and its immediate vicinity. Here and there the straining whine of the engine drew emaciated people to the roadside. They emerged from clearings in the bush, their faces haggard, their legs and arms like sticks, their scabrous bodies either shrunken about their bones or monstrously ballooned. The more desperate gesticulated, calling feebly as the Land Rover snarled by. Against his will, Richard kept going, ignoring the crying children held high almost in his path and the accusing gaze of the women who lifted them up, shame and helplessness at war within him.

A swaying wooden bridge took him across the next river. Another hour passed, an appalling hour of crablike slithering in low gear. Villages were few and far between, each as abandoned as the next. Occasionally a track filtered in, unsuitable for motorized traffic. This was the only road. Two years had gone by since Richard had volunteered for duty in the mission field and first traveled northward from Port Harcourt, but he had come this far south from time to time and was on familiar enough ground. Yet nothing seemed the same any more and every mile convinced him that the whole country must be on the brink of collapse.

The whitewashed township of Lazaru confirmed his opinion. It was well after two before he arrived and he saw at once that the place was as badly hit as Abaguma— worse, because it lacked even a medical center. Crowds pressed eagerly around the Land Rover. He had to shout above the hubbub, asking for Father O'Leary, only to learn that Tim had left two days earlier on a tour of the parish's bush villages—a stringy, bantam-weight Ibo wearing a plain blue armband volunteered the information.

"How long will he be gone?"

"Don't know, fa-da."

Richard swallowed back his disappointment. A hundred pairs of eyes were telling him, yet he asked: "What's your food position?"

"All our relief stocks are finished. What is more, fa-da, the road between here and Uziama is blocked."

Disappointment became dismay. "Are your sure?"

"Sure. I am waiting already two weeks to receive and distribute foodstuffs. That is my task."

"Who sent you?"

"Sent? No one sent. I live here and am chosen by the Holy Ghost, fa-da. But nothing come. There are landslides on the road—what else stops supplies? Lazaru will soon be dying ten a day."

Richard asked doggedly: "How far are these landslides?"

"People say six, seven miles."

"From here?"

A nod. "People say."

Rumor, always rumor. Yet, for once, it was rumor that made disastrous sense. And nobody apparently had had the strength to go and check: apathy and starvation went hand in hand. The crowd backed clear and a couple of vultures lifted heavily out of the nearest trees as Richard revved the engine.

"Fa-da O'Leary sent message north about the landslides," the Ibo claimed.

"Nothing reached us."

"He wrote to those in Abaguma."

"I'm from Abaguma," Richard retorted sharply, "and I tell you nobody brought any letter."

Went into the bush, most likely; fled, vanished. There was fear as well as chaos. Richard crashed into gear and pulled away, deaf to the cries of those who stood watching. A year ago a score of children would have chased in his wake, laughing as the mud spattered over them. Few illusions remained, but to accept defeat and turn about was out of the question. Incredibly it had taken over five hours to cover a bare nineteen miles: distances had become crazy distortions of normal time and effort, yet at least he was more than halfway to Uziama, and Uziama offered the only hope there was.

Steam rose increasingly from the hood, the tires scorched when they bit, the engine screamed. Away to the west a column of smoke hung like a waterspout. The battlefronts were shrinking, and though the war itself was still remote its side effects were everywhere. Sometimes the dead lay abandoned by the road, half-gutted, white bone and blue-black skin, but only the living had the power to move him—the famished pregnant women, the young with faces already made old, the

8

hobbling grotesques drawn into view by the sight and sound of the Land Rover.

For a brief while the slimy pot-holed surface improved slightly. The rain had lifted at last and the stifling afternoon heat burned down, sapping Richard's strength. To either side the trees gave way to deserted banana plantations and crop clearings, long since stripped bare. The road wandered through them with apparent aimlessness, a shade higher than the surrounding levels, and he was able to pick up a little speed. But not for long. The suck and slither of near bog rapidly threatened to bring him to a standstill again, and no sooner had he squelched his way clear than he met the rising ground and the earth falls.

4

Gradually the road became a narrow ledge cut into the hillside. In places the rain-loosened soil had spilled across the shelf, partially blocking progress. To begin with, Richard was able to dig a way past; a few minutes' spade work was sufficient. Fatigue throbbed in his muscles and his eyes ached from hours of concentration, but conditions weren't impossible. He had made perhaps half a mile in total isolation when he met up with a platoon of soldiers laboriously heading the other way. Only the corporal in charge wore an entire uniform and several of the men were apparently unarmed.

"How's the road back there?"

"Not good, sah."

"Can I get through?"

"On foot, sah. Not otherwise. Soon you will find no road at all." The corporal used his hands to great effect. "Broken all along."

He was right. A quarter of an hour after parting from him, Richard was confronted by a major slide. For thirty or forty yards the road had been obliterated by a solid mass of stony earth and uprooted trees—and there were further falls ahead; whole stretches of the hillside had come down. Lead seemed to fill Richard's heart as he stared at them. He had been warned, and common sense alone had told him what to expect. Frustration hammered into his fatigue. For minutes on end he gazed in utter dejection at the severed brown scar of the road snaking into the distance. With its lifeline gone, small wonder the district starved.

In the silence the vague rumble of gunfire reached him and he listened to its deep whisper with disgust. He knew something about war—and not at arm's length, as now. War had allowed him to discover what he hadn't realized he possessed—compassion, and a love of life. All war achieved was suffering. Specks wheeled in the sky beyond where the road disappeared. Death and suffering—what else? "Oh, God," he said aloud, thinking of the sisters and Albert Okawe and the long crowded huts.

"Half a miracle will do"—Albert's parting words echoed like a challenge. To return empty-handed would be unforgivable; nothing had changed. He must walk the rest of the way. At least he could stress Abaguma's plight. He might even be able to carry some of the items on the doctor's list back to the Land Rover. Beyond that his brain wouldn't function. All he knew was that at Uziama he could plead, cajole, argue. Alone he was useless. Help must come from others.

He tied a printed label to the steering column: PROPERTY OF THE SOCIETY OF THE INCARNATION, ABAGUMA. Next he made sure the petrol cap was locked. Then he collected his haversack, water flask and bush cutlass and set off, clambering over the first obstruction. The time was just after four and, at a guess, he had around ten miles to go. But it was best not to think how far it was or how long it might take or what awaited him on arrival. It was best to try not to think at all, to ignore the heat and the mud, forget that he hadn't eaten since yesterday's hash of beans.

One landslide followed another. There were stretches where the road had completely vanished between hundreds of tons of debris; others where he had to hack a way through sopping tangles of crashed trees. The road clung precariously to the slopes, rarely intact, everywhere ankle-deep in slush, and on either hand the hills gave birth to nothing but wood and leaf and rock. At one point he believed he heard the soft tearing noise of a high-flying plane, but he searched the sky for it in vain. Egyptian pilots, the radio had stated, underlining for him a private irony; Egyptian pilots, Russian aircraft.

He was far weaker than he'd realized. Slipping, falling, stumbling—as his strength ebbed a kind of light-headedness possessed him. For an immeasurable period of time he felt sick, sick at heart and sick in body, yet somehow removed from reality. Dusk was settling. He had met no one since passing the platoon heading north; the high ground was all his own. But eventually, as what remained of the road twisted down into the long wide valley where Uziama lay hidden somewhere in the evening mists, he began to find it peopled again and the awareness of disaster returned. Paths slanted in at intervals from the bush. Now, once more, there were those who also walked, lugging a few possessions, and those who could walk no further.

The dusk thickened swiftly; the insect rasp began. Fires glowed along the roadside where people crouched. The gloom spared Richard from being identified. No one cried, "Fa-da. . . . Help us, fa-da," or moved to clutch at him as he passed. A village lined the road; somewhere a bugle blared from what he took to be a military encampment. Presently he crossed the last of the rivers in a packed ferryboat, silent amid the jabbering. Never in his life could he remember being so exhausted.

Gone seven. . . . He took heart, drawing on his reserves. A scatter of early stars glinted down, but he could hardly see his way and every step jarred through to his bones. It was almost beyond belief that he had left Abaguma only that morning; the day had become everlasting. He trudged on, hemmed about by others making for the town. A soft rain suddenly set in, extinguishing the star blotches. The smell of earth and dung and death rose up anew to haunt Richard's senses. And slowly, achingly, the last mile dwindled. By seven thirty he reached the outskirts of Uziama.

What could he hope to do? . . . The question beat

11

at him as he dragged along. What could anyone do? The road would take a battalion days to clear. More and more his journey seemed an act of madness. The messengers before him must have felt the same and given up.

Somebody in uniform blundered into him at a street intersection. "The airstrip," Richard asked. "Where's the airstrip?" and followed the directions as best he could. Several trucks wallowed by, headlamps masked. Shadowy figures came and went among whitewashed houses. He made his way through the town and out the other side. The rain was no longer a drizzle. He walked with eyes narrowed, bush shirt clinging to his skin, hair plastered down. With the town behind him the road was practically invisible, but he tacked onto a man wheeling a bicycle who assured him he was also heading for the airstrip.

"Is it much farther?"

"Soon," was the grunted reply. "Soon now."

It must have gone eight before they arrived. There were no directions, no landmarks—only the obliterating darkness and the rusty croak of frogs and the irregular squelch of movement ahead and behind them along the palm-lined road. But eventually there was a single glimmer of light, then a misty suggestion of others. Before very long Richard could discern the bulk of a cluster of single-story buildings. Then all at once a barrier of oil drums confronted him and someone stepped close, someone with a rifle, helmeted and caparisoned against the rain.

"Halt! . . . Halt! . . . Nobody beyond here."

The man with the bicycle faltered. People cannoned into one another: others were squatting all around. With what command he could muster Richard said: "Let me through."

"Show your pass."

"I have no pass."

"Nobody comes through without pass," the soldier said, parrot-fashion.

"I'm a priest. I have to speak to the person in charge. It's urgent."

The soldier peered, inches away. "You from Uziama? Who you want? Church Aid?"

"Yes." Joint Church Aid. "That's right."

"They know you?"

"Yes," Richard lied, blinking into a sudden stab of torchlight.

"Okay," the soldier said uneasily after several seconds' scrutiny. "You come by."

Richard squeezed past the barrier. A gabble of protest followed him as he walked toward the largest of the buildings. "Nobody else," the soldier shouted angrily. "Stay where you are."

A few trucks were parked off to one side. Richard splashed through mud to the yellow slits which framed a door, fumbled for the handle, pushed and entered.

He found himself in a room about thirty feet square, lit by hurricane lamps. It had perhaps a dozen occupants, three or four of whom were in uniform—he saw a colored nurse, a couple of army officers. All eyes were on him as he tried to take in the scene, but it was the thin, shirt-sleeved, middleaged man nearest the door who spoke.

"Who the devil are you?" he exclaimed. "And where the blazes did you spring from?"

CHAPTER TWO

1

Richard wiped the rain from his face. "Abaguma."

"That's to the north," someone said from the far corner.

"North, south, east—who cares? How the hell did this guy get in here?"

Cigarette smoke stung Richard's eyes. "Your guard let me through."

"Isn't that just fine?" The man wheeled indignantly on one of the Ibo officers. "Captain, where's the blind use in having a checkpoint out there? For God's sake go and make it clear that we aren't a port of call for anyone who happens by."

"I was asked for my pass," Richard said.

"Have you got one?"

"No."

"You see?" the man snapped at the captain, who picked up a raincoat and limped outside.

"The guard's not to blame," Richard said. "I told him I knew you."

"Since when?"

Apart from a couple of tables and a few chairs the room was bare. Richard's legs were shaking. His body throbbed from end to end and he swayed as if he were drunk.

"You a priest?" the man asked doubtfully, studying him. He had the toneless accent of the Eastern seaboard of America.

Richard nodded.

"You could have fooled me."

Richard leaned against the table in front of him. "Are you in charge here?"

"Not exactly."

"Who is?"

"My job's to coordinate relief work in the area, if that's what you mean."

Richard glared. "I haven't traveled all day for someone to start splitting hairs." His voice shook. "There are three or four thousand people in and around Abaguma. They need food, they need drugs—"

"What d'you expect from me?" the man interjected. "Tears?" He was ashen, nervy, hostile—all from strain. "Listen," he said, jabbing a finger toward the door. "They're starving out there as well, or didn't you notice? Draw a ten-mile circle from where you stand and you'll find fifty thousand in the self-same boat. Starvation, fever, kwashiorkor, dysentery—you name it, they've got it, and the poor bastards are going like flies. We can't even cope with the area we're meant to sustain. A couple of plane-loads a night are almost as useless as nothing at all. Peanuts."

He paused and rubbed his beard stubble. When he spoke again it was with a shrug of regret. "Help from this quarter as far as you're concerned is a nonstarter. I'm sorry, but that's the situation, and it's better you know it right away." His mouth flicked involuntarily as he held Richard's gaze. "I'm sorry," he repeated. "You're not the first to ask, but we've got tragedy enough of our own."

Without pausing he called sharply: "Any word yet, Lenny?"

Someone answered from a side room: "Not up to now."

"Try them again, for God's sake. Keep trying."

Richard felt his legs going. He lurched along the length of the table and collapsed onto a chair, head in hands, failure and exhaustion beating behing the blood-red darkness of his closed eyes. Presently he was touched on the shoulder.

"Scotch, father?" It was the nurse. He found himself clasping a plastic mug. "Looks as if you could do with it."

He straightened and gulped the whiskey down. For a second or two the room blurred and the rain seemed to drum louder on the corrugated iron roof.

"How far's this place you're from?" the thin American was asking.

"Between thirty and forty miles."

"Can you make it back all right? I mean—what's your transport situation? If you're low on gas, or if maybe—"

"The road's gone," Richard said. "Landslides."

"You walked?"

"The last third."

The American stood clicking a thumbnail against his teeth. Static crackled in the side room. "There's no other route?"

"No."

"So didn't you realize you were bound to finish up a loser? No road means no supplies—that's the basic equation the way things are. Even if we were flowing with milk and honey that's how it would be. Didn't it ever cross your mind?"

Richard gestured weakly. An insect pinged against the nearest lamp and spiraled to the floor; there was no end to dying. He unbuttoned one of the pockets in the bush shirt and drew out Albert Okawe's list. The ink had run on the sopping paper.

"There was always this," he heard himself saying. "I told myself I could at least manage something—medicines if not food, certain items if not others, depending on what was available."

The American's face was expressionless as he ran his eyes over the blurred scrawl. "Nothing's available."

Hope outlasts reason. "Nothing in reserve? Nothing at all? Surely—"

"Reserve?" The tone was scornful. "With people dropping on our doorstep? Be realistic, father. Within an hour of a plane touching down we're cleaned out. Last night we had two deliveries—around seven tons in all." As if he believed Richard doubted him, the American snatched a clip of papers from the table. "Maize, beans, oil, dried and canned fish, protein concentrates, vitamin concentrates, salt, antibiotics, antimalarial drugs," he read at a rattle, then looked up. "All allocated in advance, all trucked away to distribution points. And tonight will be the same—*if* we get a plane in, that is. Tonight and every night. . . . This isn't Uli. This is a soft earth strip. Reserves? Seven tons are like so many crumbs." He flung the clip down in disgust. "If I had as much as a spare pack of aspirin left laying around I wouldn't be fit to be here. None of us would."

Limping, the Ibo captain let himself back into the hut. A rhythmless dirge sounded from the darkness while the door was open.

"Listen to 'em," the American said. "Listen to the poor devils," and went into the side room as if to escape.

With a kind of heartbreak Richard stared at the flag pins stuck in a map on the opposite wall. The cupped

16

hands, the fevered appeals—now he knew what it was like to be personally denied.

2

He leaned back in the chair with his eyes shut, sunk within himself. Desperation had blinded him. The hours-long proof of areawide catastrophe had somehow failed to underline that no matter how much he begged and argued it would be in vain. Abaguma had no special claims. He had nothing new to shock with, nothing to touch and move the springs of mercy in tired men: death and the degradation of the living were a commonplace.

"You know what you're asking?" the American had said. "You're asking me to sacrifice people here so that you can perhaps save a few where you come from—don't you see? That's what it amounts to. All I've got is loaves and fishes, father, loaves and fishes."

So it had been impossible to beg, useless to argue. Richard stirred fretfully, body burning with fatigue, mind close to tears. His clothes steamed, warm and clinging against his skin. The wireless crackled spasmodically in the next room and all about him there was constant activity, the clash and murmur of voices, the mounting tension of waiting. But he himself was ignored. He was an interloper, faced with nothing but the destitute return journey that had been so unthinkable.

Suddenly he was aware that the voices had quickened. "Just the one?" he heard.

"That's all. George Sharkey's Constellation."

"What's happened to Bodelsen?"

"God knows."

"Have we got Sharkey's ETA?"

"Twenty-three fifteen."

"And the load?" someone asked with a German-type accent.

"Mixture as before. Without Bodelsen we'll have to reallocate."

Richard sat up and glanced at his watch. The thin American crossed to one of the sacking-covered windows

17

and peered out at the rain. "Oh hell," he muttered to the second of the Ibo officers. "D'you figure it might lift?"

"Perhaps." The tone was fatalistic.

"You're a comfort, I must say." Raw-eyed, he turned to Richard. "It'll be like a mud bath out there." Coming closer and offering a cigarette, he said: "I'd wait till morning if I were you. You can't set off in this. Wait till morning—you won't be under our feet." He lit both their cigarettes. *Thirty-five?* he wondered as the flame emphasized the structure of Richard's wasted face. "I'm sorry," he said once more, and the ironed-out voice carried genuine sympathy. "I guess I know how you must feel."

Richard lifted his shoulders; let them drop. He hadn't smoked in over a month and his vision rocked. An idea half entered his mind. "This Constellation—where's it from?"

"São Tomé. A two-hour shuttle, doglegging all the way and never the same route twice. Sharkey brings in around four tons. A full payload's impossible with the size and quality of strip we have to offer."

"Does he return empty?"

"Mostly."

"Is there anything to stop him taking me?"

"Your own common sense, mainly. What d'you hope to gain? Sharkey would probably agree, lift-off conditions permitting—but for what?" A shake of the head. "Forget it, father."

"Where else are planes landing?"

"Nowhere near here. Not any more. A start was made at Ogua Ngwa, but an Ilyushin soon put paid to that."

There was a pause, a string of vivid cameos flitting across Richard's mind. He pushed himself stiffly to his feet. Albert was right; Abaguma would rot. "I can't give up now."

"Listen," the American said (Richard was never to know his name). "It took ten days to hack this strip, such as it is, out of the bush. Nobody just waved a wand. We're a JCA venture, which means full backing. Even so, there's a limit to what can be done. What d'you expect to achieve on your own? Wherever you go and

18

whichever relief organization you go to, the problem's the same. Without local landing facilities you haven't a chance." A jet of smoke ballooned and curled. "I'm telling you, not a chance. Look at us here—we've been operating almost a week, but with too little and too late. Every goddamn thing's against keeping many of these people alive."

"A strip isn't essential. Stuff can be free-dropped."

"It's not that easy." Amateurs were forever making impractical suggestions. "There are dozens of factors—the lie of the land, aircraft availability. . . . Besides, it's like I told you before—anything put in would probably be at the expense of somewhere else."

Richard's nostrils flared. "Abaguma's been denied from the beginning."

"All right. But they aren't magicians on the offshore islands, or anywhere else. Uli apart, there's only one other strip functioning. Abaguma's not alone in going short."

"Short!"

"I'm only trying to paint the picture," the American said, strain hard held. "Let me put it this way. What's so different about you if you fetch up in São Tomé? What special line will you have to sell? And what authority for selling it?"

"I'm responsible for my parish."

"You'll find that cuts damn-all ice in São Tomé. Biafra's going to hell in a handbasket and the relief agencies have got every other guy tugging at their sleeves down there—all with good urgent cause. D'you reckon they'll so much as notice you?"

"That's a risk I must take."

"God," the American said slowly, "you're as stubborn as they come," and turned away shaking his head.

3

With an air of determination Richard folded Albert's list and shoved it into his shirt pocket. How he would get back to where he belonged he couldn't imagine, but the personal consequences must wait, everything else must take its turn.

He buttoned the pocket down and began to pace the floor, caught in the whirl of decision. It would be a crime not to go on; there was nothing to be lost, perhaps everything to gain. . . . The room had quietened and he scorned the patience of the others. Time seemed to have slowed to a crawl. Ten forty-five came and went before those in the room with him at last began to rouse themselves. The nurse had already gone outside, but now others prepared to leave. Yawning, the civilian with the German accent heeled out his cigarette.

"What d'you say?" he asked the American, who nodded.

"May as well get the trucks in position, yeah. . . ." To the Ibo captain the American said: "Don't start lighting the flare path, John—understood? There'll be no intruders in this weather but we're running low on kerosene. Time enough for the flares when Sharkey's within earshot."

The two officers donned their raincoats and left. In the darkness one of them could be heard shouting orders. The American came over to Richard. "Surely you've changed your mind?"

"No."

"Have you got a passport?"

"No."

"Health card?"

"No," Richard gritted.

"They'll expect them in São Tomé."

"That's a bridge I'll worry about when I come to it."

A grimace, lips pursed. "I can give you a Caritas flight pass: something's better than nothing. But remember—it's up to Sharkey whether you go or not."

"I quite understand."

"Are you dried out yet?"

"After a fashion."

"You'll freeze at altitude. I'll see what I can do about something warm."

"Thanks. You're very kind."

20

"It may not be the best of rides." Quizzically, the American added: "I suppose you've flown before?"

"Oh yes."

The past was of no consequence. The American came back from the side room with a baggy old cardigan and a length of oilskin which Richard draped across his shoulders. The trucks outside were retching into life, drawing away.

"Bring a lamp, somebody."

The American crossed to the door, followed by three colleagues; Richard went last into the night. The rain was down to a drizzle and the moaning of the crowd squatting invisibly beyond the checkpoint had died to an expectant murmur. The American turned right and led a way between the huts, the ground squashing under foot.

"Rather him than me," one of the men grunted, and Richard knew he was referring to the pilot. They traipsed on for several hundred yards: here and there the surface was scored with ruts, everywhere grassless and glistening in the swinging lamp's glow. Ahead of them the trucks had already been maneuvered into a row, headlights dipped; vaguely Richard could distinguish a line of white-ringed canisters flanking each side of the strip.

When they reached the trucks the group took shelter. There were five trucks in all, equally spaced, pointed head-on down the strip. The drivers were army men: they crouched beneath the nearest tailboard, binding lengths of rag to bayonet-long wooden sticks. The smell of kerosene was unmistakable. "Where's the child?" the American asked nobody in particular.

"Under cover," the junior of the officers answered, "with the nurse. She's all right."

"Child?" Richard frowned.

The American nodded. "Dumped on us with a label around her neck. God knows who by, or quite how. Right on our doorstep—literally. According to the label the whole family was wiped out in the bombing raid on Ogua Ngwa."

"How old?"

21

"Two? Less, probably. Best thing's to get her away if we can. At least she'll have a future. The alternative's to put her back in the ruck with the rest. Generally the adults don't want to go, even when they're on their last legs, and they won't be separated from their kids. Perhaps it's just as well. We'd be stampeded otherwise, and a plane would never come unstuck from this glue pot with anything like a load. It barely gets thirteen hundred yards—and that's stretching it."

The rain was falling with a soggy hiss. They stood around in silence. Once in a while the child's muffled voice could be heard from inside one of the driving cabs, and to Richard it sounded as if it were wailing not only for itself but for everyone the world had harmed and would harm yet. He leaned against the side of a truck, thoughts focusing grimly on Abaguma, and a kind of panic began to gnaw at his renewed resolve. "You're too impetuous, Richard. Far too impetuous"—his father's complaint intruded from the past, an unwanted reminder. He had merely tasted failure, not swallowed it whole. There was still time to reconsider. He was a priest, and Abaguma needed him as a priest. . . . Then the child cried again, crying out of terror and need and abandonment, and the pendulum swung in Richard's mind. The sisters would understand, Albert would understand. Man couldn't live by prayer alone; the evidence was all about them and their special calling acknowledged it. . . .

"Listen!"

Richard jerked his face to the sky; everyone did. A mosquito's whine, the rain's whisper. But nothing else.

"I could have sworn. . . ."

They were like statues, heads cocked, breath held. Still nothing. For seconds on end nothing. Then someone else spoke, gruff with certainty: "I have it. Over there. . . ."

Almost simultaneously Richard heard a groan throb lazily in from the west.

"That's Sharkey. That'll be him," the American said, as matter-of-fact as ever. "Light up, for Christ's sake, before he overshoots."

4

The trucks' headlamps were snapped to full beam. The soldiers stumbled forward with their guttering torches. Canister by canister the strip lengthened as gouts of oily flame began to flap at regular intervals. An excited gabble came from the crowd massed at the checkpoint and through it the sound of the plane ebbed and flowed elusively, seeming to come from several directions at once.

"Sod these clouds," somebody muttered.

The strip was about a third lit, tunneling a rain-blurred glow through the darkness.

"Reckon he's got us?"

No one answered. Richard shielded his face, eyes screwed. He pivoted slowly, searching the sky to the northwest, judging the plane to be on the turn. It was low, that much was certain, uncomfortably low. No aids, no ceiling; he remembered how it was to grope one's way. . . . Gradually the beat of the engines became more constant, guttural, pierced with traces of a scream. North now, north and still coming around. A minute or two elapsed. At last the strip was burning from end to end.

"Attaboy, Sharkey. . . . Come on, fellah. . . ."

And almost immediately the Constellation burst into view, shabby, scudding through the murk, belly light winking. The triple tail plane was unmistakable. It roared diagonally above the parked trucks with deafening suddenness, drowning the ragged cheer that rose in greeting. Sharkey rocked the wings from side to side as if he were flying a fighter. At less than a thousand feet he banked sharply to port and swung away to circle wide for his approach. Then, as swiftly as it had appeared, the plane was erased. For minutes on end it thundered unseen, the roar crumbling, playing tricks, until slowly it built to a crescendo again, homing in from the south.

When they saw it a second time the wheels were already lowered. Throttled back, the Constellation skimmed toward the far end of the flare path, ghostlike yet cumbersome, dropping fast. It wobbled once, as if Sharkey had almost lost his line, but as early as he could be smacked it down; even from where the trucks were they saw the mud spurt. The tail started to slew immediately, but he ruddered and held it straight. As the nose wheel made contact the plane lurched madly, but again Sharkey somehow kept control, braking hard, slithering plumb between the flares in a great arc of spray.

His handling was superb. He couldn't waste a yard. With scarcely a quarter mile of strip to spare it was touch and go whether he would overrun, but he was slowing all the time, slowing fast, wheels plowing the mud. Two hundred yards from the trucks and he was down to a comparative crawl, outer engines feathered. Still losing momentum, the plane nosed into range of the headlamps and trundled to within a stone's throw of the waiting group. Little danger now; a novice could do the rest. Yet when Sharkey finally jerked to a standstill and shut the engines, their dying whine was like a sigh of relief.

Everyone started to move, as if a spell had been broken. The drivers scrambled into their trucks and raced them over to the dirt-spattered plane, backing in close to the rear doors.

"Let's go." The American motioned to Richard.

They heaved themselves inside by way of a truck's hood. The long tube of the fuselage was waist-high with cargo; several soldiers were already cutting it loose and beginning to heave the stuff out. Richard and the American clanked through to the cockpit between walls of roped crates and gunny bags. The stink of stockfish dominated everything else.

"Hi, George."

"Hallo, yourself." An Australian.

"Had us biting our nails as usual."

"You weren't the only ones."

"Never figured you'd have us in your sights so soon."

"I've got a flaming marvel of a navigator, that's why."

"Hi, Frank. . . . Great job tonight—real great."

"Thanks."

24

Richard peered into the cockpit from behind the American. Bald, squat, loose-jowled—Sharkey wasn't a conventional picture of courage. At least fifty—and his campanion couldn't have been all that much younger. Chewing, Sharkey stretched himself and scratched his rust-red sideburns.

"Any trouble on the way?" the American asked.

"Not a mouse stirring."

"Why isn't Bodelsen making a run?"

"Cracked his landing gear. Nothing serious. He'll be in business again tomorrow."

"A single load is a drop in the ocean. It hardly—"

"Thanks," Sharkey said dryly. "See how welcome we are, Frank?"

"Lengthen the strip and you'll get more visitors," the navigator said, rubbing his eyes. Scottish, this one; Glasgow or thereabouts. "Some of the other fellows would be willing to chance their arm. Everyone else plumps for Uli—and I can't say I blame 'em."

"Give us time. We're doing all we can."

As the fuselage deck was emptied the urgent scrape and clatter grew more resonant. Sacking dust thickened the air.

"Here's your checklist." Oozing sweat, Sharkey handed over some papers, one of which the American signed and passed back. "Plus the usual," Sharkey added. "Strictly medicinal." Two bottles of scotch. He grinned weakly, loose-chinned. "When the moon's right we'll try making a double trip. Bodelsen's willing, too. . . . That'll help, eh?"

"Sure will," the American nodded. Until then he seemed to have forgotten Richard's existence. "By the way—how d'you feel about passengers?"

"After last night?"

"Only two."

"Last night we almost clipped the trees."

"Only two—and one's a kid."

"Last night they were all kids. And we weren't sitting on a marsh, like now."

"Only two, George," the American repeated.

Sharkey chewed his lower lip. "No more?"

"You'll never notice them."

A long pause, professionalism behind the apparent callousness. "All right. If we must, I suppose." Slewing in his seat, Sharkey saw Richard for the first time. "You, is it?"

"Plus the child."

"Your responsibility? Sorry, but I don't want to be lumbered back at base with a stray."

Richard glanced at the American, who said: "Save the Children will take her over on arrival."

"All right, then," Sharkey agreed. "Sold."

A series of heavy thumps sounded from the rear and someone shouted: "Everything's out."

"Shall I get the girl?" Richard asked.

"Yeah, do that," the American answered. "We're almost through."

Richard walked back along the empty deck and clambered down onto the tailboard of a truck; the last few sacks were being stowed. It was spitting with rain and the clamor of the crowd over by the huts was louder and uglier in its hunger than before. He dropped to the ground and went to the driving cab, where the nurse sat cradling the child. "Is she going?" the nurse asked and he nodded, taking the girl awkwardly into his possession. She was all bones, thumb in mouth, eyes half closed, even lighter than he'd expected, and she wore a stained, knee-length cotton dress, as plain as a shroud. Written in ink on the label tied to one wrist was MARCIA EMEZIE OF OGUA NGWA.

"I think she'll sleep soon," the nurse said. "Good-bye, little one."

Richard walked back to the Constellation. To one of the truck drivers he said: "Give me a leg-up will you?"

The American was coming aft as Richard stumbled aboard. "I'll keep my fingers crossed for you, father."

"Thanks."

"Good-bye." His handshake was firm and encouraging but his expression reiterated that, in his view, Richard hadn't a hope in a million. Then he looked at the child and the set of his face softened; the hard shell was transparently thin. "Given luck she won't remember. I reckon that's about the best one can wish for her—lousy, isn't it?"

An intensity of feeling swept Richard. Momentarily he was tongue-tied: the world was never meant to be like this. " 'Bye," he managed and watched the American go out of his life.

"Come and join us," Sharkey was calling.

He turned and went forward. The heat was stifling and the stink of dried fish still lingered. Sharkey introduced his co-pilot and navigator. "Frank—Frank Izzard."

"Richard Lawrence."

"Who's the kid? Anyone special?"

"They're all special."

Only exhaustion could have make him so smug. He saw the two men exchange glances. "*Touché*," Sharkey said evenly.

The first of the loaded trucks was pulling away: Sharkey jerked a thumb aft. "Seal the doors, Frank, and we'll get the blazes out of here." Then, to Richard: "Gather you haven't any papers—right?"

"A flight pass, that's all."

"Not to worry." Again that flabby grin. "Rules were made for fools." Twisting around, he indicated four inward-facing bucket seats to the rear of the cockpit. "Take your choice. And hang on—this strip's real switchback and the old crate's a bit weak at the knees. But don't be alarmed. Once she's up where she belongs she goes like a bird."

5

Richard subsided into one of the seats and settled the child across his lap. Sharkey and Izzard were going through their takeoff drill and he was too played out to be interested. Presently, one by one, Sharkey fired the engines, ran them together under advancing throttle until the plane shook, then eased them down and began to taxi to the far end of the strip. It undulated gently, as if they were heading into a slow swell. Where the last pair of flares fluttered like rags in the rain, Sharkey brought the Constellation around in a tight half-circle and made his alignment. Only then did Richard brace himself.

Sharkey wasn't one to waste time: without delay he put on power. Braked, the plane began to shudder again. The roar was deafening and the child opened her mouth in a renewal of fear, the cry inaudible. Richard could feel the tail straining to lift, but Sharkey kept the plane tethered, needing all the initial momentum he could get. Then with a sudden lurch the brakes were released and they shot violently forward, gathering speed between the flares, bucking over the atrocious surface.

The ground began to race by in a glistening smear. Richard shot a sidelong glance at Sharkey. Three-quarters of a mile maximum; silently he urged up the speed. "Eighty knots," Izzard called. One stomach-tugging undulation followed another in quick succession before the ground ran fairly level. "Hundred knots. . . . Hundred and ten. . . ." Izzard's voice grew crisper. The spaced flares were blurring together at last, but they didn't extend forever; the truck's headlights were massed only three, four hundred yards ahead. But still Sharkey delayed—a few seconds more yet long enough for Richard's neck hair to bristle.

"Hundred and thirty—"

At the last instant Sharkey pulled back on the stick and they lost contact. In a shallow climb the plane swept heavily above the trucks, up and over the glimmer that was Uziama, swinging to port, wheels thudding home as they gained height. Turning in his harness, Sharkey grinned triumphantly at Izzard, telltale beads of sweat dribbling down his face. "How about that, then?" And Izzard grimaced as if in disbelief.

Richard sucked in a deep breath; his nerves were out of practice. Obliquely below to their left the flare path was already being extinguished. Soon it was gone, blotted out by thick cloud. The Constellation jolted through a series of bumps: for minutes on end they were lashed with rain and there was nothing to be seen. Then, abruptly, they soared clear and the vast dome of the sky was quivering with stars.

Sharkey altered pitch, leveling off only a little above

the cloud cover. Richard settled painfully against the metal sheeting supporting the bucket seat. The child had stopped crying and he held her close. Soon, like her, he slept. His head lolled sideways and his lips parted as he sank deeper and deeper into unconsciousness. But even in the depths there was no escape. Sister Marie was waiting there for him, gaunt beyond words, asking "When will you be back?" And he twitched in the seat, unable to answer.

CHAPTER THREE

1

The stars were still there when Richard woke, but the rain clouds had disappeared: perhaps five thousand feet below the sea lay wrinkled in the blue-black night. He was cold and moved stiffly, shifting the weight of the child in his arms, haunted anew by memories and apprehensions. The girl lay across him like a doll, the small face peaceful in oblivion, her bones sharp and fragile against his own.

Almost two o'clock. . . . His watch was loose on his wrist. Bleary-eyed, he gazed back along the tunnel of the fuselage. There was tremendous vibration, as if power drills were at work, and air leaked through the battered inner cladding. Aching, he moved position again, pulling the length of oilskin closer around his shoulders, and this time Izzard noticed him stir.

"Okay?"

"Thanks," Richard nodded.

"Do with a bite?"

"It can wait."

Izzard must have misheard because he passed him a meat sandwich, following it with a mug of sweetened tea which he slopped from a flask. Empty though he was, Richard seemed to have gone beyond hunger: the tea was warm and welcome but the coarse moist bread stuck in his throat.

"How soon will we be down?" He had to shout.

"Twenty minutes." This was Sharkey. "You'll see the place before long."

"And then?"

"Shut-eye. . . . Have you got anywhere fixed?"

"No."

"You can share our room if you want. Might as well, you know. The town's all but dead from now until dawn." He made a small correction to the stick as the plane wallowed slightly. "Who d'you want to see?"

"Anyone and everyone."

"It's like a madhouse most of the time. Babel— you've no idea. Aid groups galore—left, right and center."

Munching, Izzard frowned. "Are you just trying your luck?"

"You could say that."

"Where are you from? Near Uziama?"

"Further north."

"Is it much the same there?"

How often, Richard wondered dully, would he be asked? Abaguma wouldn't have reached the headlines. And how did he even begin to answer?

"We haven't a road any more, let alone a landing strip. You can probably guess what that means."

Sharkey took over. "There's stuff rotting by the ton on the docks and in the airfield bays. The problem is to deliver it. With the best will in the world I don't see how you're going to get relief to your area without ground—"

"I want supplies free-dropped."

"That's not as easy as it sounds."

"So I've been told."

Richard clenched his jaws. He could but try; try and

30

try again. Someone might listen, someone with the authority and the will to act.

Izzard broke the urgent stream of his thoughts. "There she blows." Straightening, Richard could make out a dark, irregular mass strewn patchily with lights: it was almost dead ahead, broad and solid-looking against the star-shimmer of the ribbed sea. Sharkey altered course, heeling a shade to port, then leveled. Izzard gave him speed and altitude before turning to Richard.

"Don't worry yourself about documentation when we land. We'll see you're cleared. They're pretty lax."

"Thanks." The child moved in Richard's arms as if horror wasn't far away. "How long have you been with Joint Church Aid?"

"Six weeks or so."

"What brought you into it?"

"The money," Izzard answered unashamedly. "Does that shake you?"

"No."

"Plus the fact that George and I were going spare. The independent we flew for went bust."

They were beginning to lose height. Richard's ears suddenly clogged and he barely heard Sharkey. "Some of the aid crews have made a career out of other people's troubles. Wars, earthquakes, floods—name the place and the year and they were there. Frank and me—we're filling in, earning a worthwhile penny. The same goes for most of the others too, though a few would carry anything if they had the chance and the terms were right. Currently, of course, weapons are the thing—guns, ammunition and such like. If what we hear's correct that's mostly routed through Libreville and Cotonou. But São Tomé isn't all it seems. On the surface it's the biggest charity base in the world, but what goes on out of public sight can sometimes stink. Politics, cranks, jealousies, pressure groups, bribes, threats, promises. . . . They're all on the buzz, believe me. It's been an eye-opener, hasn't it, Frank?"

"You bet."

Richard shook his head in despair: isolation must have made him naïve. The diseased and the starving and the

31

hundreds already laid on their backs in the wet ground at Abaguma deserved better. Instinctively his arms gathered around the sleeping child. He shivered, conscious of the cold again, and stared without expression between the heads of the two men, watching the island take shape.

2

Chewing still, Sharkey brought the Constellation around seaward of black, precipitous mountains. He flew the plane with absolute assurance, coming in close under the lee of the peaks, closer than many would have thought wise.

Far out on the water a ship was heading eastward; nearer in, a few fishing boats winked their lamps. Sharkey swung northward himself, steady at three thousand feet, leaving the mountains behind. The island opened up, shelving down to broad expanses of rain forest. Beyond the sheen of the forest and its twisting rivers the land flattened almost completely, and Richard could decipher crisscrossed patterns of cultivation encrusted with villages. They swept in, bucking a little. The broken strands of light that hinted at plantation roads webbed increasingly together in the far northwest, merging into a diffused pinkish glow.

"São Tomé town," Sharkey announced for Richard's benefit. "Tell 'em we're here, Frank—as if they didn't know."

Izzard called control, requesting permission to land. It was all very perfunctory. "Okay, and thanks," he signed off, and nodded to Sharkey. A minute later he said: "Gear coming down." There was a thud as the wheels locked. "Gear down. . . . Two thousand feet, one hundred and seventy knots."

Sharkey was homing on a straight bright streamer to the west of the town. Izzard continued to guide him in, their exchanges less casual, more terse, as if their nerves were niggling at last. Fifteen hundred feet, the concrete runway suddenly clear, pale gray between the shining markers. A thousand feet, five hundred. . . . Thirty-degree flaps, the runway absolutely centered on the nose and the ground beginning to disclose details to either side.

"Three hundred," Izzard warned.

"Got it."

Flaps advanced to sixty degrees. Low trees, a ring of fuel tanks, the striped aiming point on the runway, the red flash-flash of a beacon. Sharkey had the old plane exactly right: he stroked the wheels onto the oil-slicked surface in a caress. After Uziama it must have seemed like child's play. They ran with a jarring whine past the squat control tower, then turned and taxied slowly to the dispersal area.

Sharkey yawned as he cut the engines. "How's the kid?" he asked, unclipping his harness.

"Still asleep."

"Lucky so-and-so." He looked suddenly played out, older, looser under the jaw. "Sorry, father—reckon that wasn't the cleverest thing to say. Let's hope she's expected. Otherwise it'll be like trying to deliver a wrongly addressed letter—and this is no hour to start bollocking around playing postman."

3

The airport was ringed with warehouses, some ablaze with light and attended by trucks. Several twin-engined aircraft squatted like mosquitoes to left and right of the apron. Beyond, a DC 4 was being fueled, and beyond it again Richard could make out at least two Constellations taking on loads.

The heat was sweltering. He walked behind Sharkey and Izzard, the child awake again but silent, her body tensed. They entered the main building block by way of a side door and the sudden brightness made Richard shield his eyes. Sharkey led them along a peeling corridor that brought them into a square central area fenced by immigration and customs barriers. Knots of people waited in the space beyond. Their voices and those of the uniformed officials murmured off the high, fan-churning ceiling.

Sharkey nodded to the swarthy, capless man who offered a thin smile of recognition as they reached immigration. There were no separate channels for air crews, no apparent concessions, though a familiar face seemed as acceptable as any document.

"Constellation," Sharkey said affably, as if it were a password. "Joint Church Aid, Uziama."

The man stamped the proffered papers without perusal. "Okay."

Sharkey added a winning smile. "Don't you ever go to bed, *amigo?*"

Bad teeth, uncomprehending eyes. "Fly good?"

"Great."

Sharkey was through the gate, Izzard too, when the man checked them. "The others?" He indicated Richard and the child.

"They're with us."

"Not crew." The accent was thick, the vocabulary limited. "Not same like you. . . . Passport?" he asked Richard, eyeing the scarecrow clothes.

"Forget it," Izzard cut in. "He's a priest, and the girl is—"

"Priest?" The word carried an uplift of doubt.

"Priest, yes. Come on, *amigo*," Sharkey snapped. "You know what's happening over there. They gave him a flight pass, a Caritas flight pass, but they waived the rest—which is what you'll do." Without attempt at subtlety he pulled out some paper money and flipped a couple of notes across the counter. "They're hardly tourists, are they, *amigo?* Look at 'em."

The man shrugged. Money argued best of all. "Okay," he said and motioned Richard by.

"Idiot," Sharkey muttered once they were clear.

Customs was a formality. Sharkey and Izzard were greeted with nods. The only question was for Richard. "Anything?" a wiry, blue-jowled Portuguese inquired, cigarette between lips, and Sharkey answered: "All he's got is a hollow belly. . . . *Adeus.* See you fellows again tomorrow—yes?"

A young pink-cheeked woman crossed to meet them as they left the barrier. She wore an identification disc on her blouse: MISS SUSAN GABLE, SAVE THE CHILDREN FUND. "Are you from the Uziama Constellation—the plane just in?" She took Izzard's confirmation in her stride. "So this is Marcia, is it? Marcia Emezie?"

"That's right."

"Poor thing." She tickled the child gently under the chin, smiling into the small, wizened face. "Hallo, sweet. Hallo, Marcia. We'll soon have you tucked in bed and your troubles will all be over." Her voice was briskly efficient. "How old?" she asked Richard.

"Two, perhaps less. All that's known about her is on the label."

"Poor thing."

She relieved Richard of the child with practiced ease. MARCIA EMEZIE OF OGUA NGWA: the baggage of some of those who waited nearby was more decoratively tagged. Not all flights were mercy flights; São Tomé still managed a life of its own. People stared in bovine fashion, curious, ignorant of the starving children held high in appeal by frantic mothers along the road from Abaguma, ignorant of so much, ignorant and blameless and unmoved. Disaster happened elsewhere; never to you and yours, never closer than nearby.

On the way to the exit Sharkey said to Miss Gable, "We're taking a taxi. Can we drop you somewhere?"

"Thanks, but I have a car."

The night was still and humid. Someone detached himself from a dark corner and sidled up to Sharkey. "You want a watch, captain?"

"Beat it!"

Another world was closing in. Miss Gable said, "Well, good-night. Good-night everyone." A Volkswagen was by the curb, jacketless driver at the wheel. Izzard opened the door and Miss Gable ducked inside, hugging the child, smiling goodnight again as she sat back. Seconds later they were watching the car draw away and, despite the dead weight of body and mind, Richard experienced a momentary pang of deprivation.

They boarded the taxi first in line—an old Chevrolet convertible with broken fenders. Sharkey gave the address. The three of them sat abreast, the top down, the

35

air hot against their skin even as they gathered speed. At the airport's perimeter they passed a military control post. The road swung wide and for about half a mile ran beside a high wire fence, in front of which soldiers patrolled and beyond which were the crammed warehouses, the poised aircraft. .

Richard turned his gaze away. The road pointed between twin rows of palms, their heads like static shrapnel bursts. The airport fell behind, its place taken by shadowy levels of crops and irrigation channels; but these didn't last for long. The capital came at them quicker than Richard anticipated—first the tatty outskirts where it ran untidily to seed, and then the colonial stucco of the downtown avenues.

"There isn't a Hilton," Sharkey said. "Frank and I rent a room in a boarding house. But we can easily fit you in. No problem. Anyway, you'd never find somewhere for yourself—and that's not because of the time of night. Tomé's hardly more than an overgrown village and it's bursting at the seams."

They half-circled a statue and turned into an unlit street.

"Another thing." Now it was Izzard. "How are you off for cash?"

Pride belonged to the past. Richard managed a rueful smile, a shrug of acceptance. He was dropping.

Sharkey chuckled. Then sharply to the driver: "Here, sport! On the right! . . . Here—yes. . . . Yes."

Richard followed Izzard and Sharkey from the car. Vaguely he was conscious of a star-blanched façade, a porch-covered entrance and moths flattened like arrowheads around a wall light. The taxi snarled off down the street. Izzard was first up the porch steps; he held the front door open with his foot to let Richard and Sharkey inside. A staircase slanted out of the lobby—cane chairs, an ornate mirror, some thick-leafed plants. There was a spiced smell.

"Just the one floor." Sharkey had Richard's measure.

The stairs creaked. The room was L-shaped, untidy and stifling. Wardrobe, chest of drawers, two beds and a couch. A calendar nude hung askew on one of the plain walls, a fly-blown print on another. Sharkey flung the shutters wide.

"Use the bed on the left."

Richard shook his head. "The couch will be fine."

"The bed," Sharkey insisted. "Don't argue, for God's sake—not at three in the morning. You've got troubles enough."

Richard was wilting fast. His voice didn't sound like his own any more. "If that's how you want it," he said lamely.

The bed seemed to rise to meet him as he slumped, its sagging springs and worn mattress the softest combination he'd ever known. He plummeted into sleep the instant his body came to rest and never felt Sharkey unlace and remove his mud-caked boots or drop the mosquito netting.

4.

When he woke, blinking into the morning's angled light, he couldn't immediately recall where he was. It took a few bleary seconds for the realization to hit him and the past twenty-four hours to jigsaw together. He sat up stiffly and clasped his bent knees, remaining hunched and motionless as if he were nursing a wound, his mind churning, heedless of Izzard's whistling snore and Sharkey's half-naked bulk.

Eventually, out of the corner of his eye, he became aware of something propped on the bedside table. *If you want to start early*, he read, *go ahead. We sleep like drunks. Bathroom's across the corridor. Use my razor, and what's under it. Places to eat are in the main avenue. Good luck, and come back here if it suits. Always welcome—Sharkey*. An electric razor was also on the table, weighing down some paper money: a thousand escudos. Moved, Richard counted out the worn notes. A priest begged more than most, but the unexpected kindnesses were the ones that swelled the heart. For a long moment he looked at Sharkey's gaping mouth and fleshy features; no one was ever quite what he

37

seemed to be. Then he got up, took the razor and went quietly into the bathroom, shaved and showered.

Putting on his stained clothes blunted the feeling of freshness, though not his hunger; he was dizzy from it. The others were still sleeping when he reentered their room to check and memorize Sharkey's scrawled afterthought—*The address is 12 Rua da Veronica.* He could find nothing to write with; thanks must wait. He pocketed the money and tiptoed down the stairs. In the street he kicked most of the dried mud from his boots, then started toward the avenue. The air was warm and musty, the street empty except for a couple of scavenging dogs. The houses were tight-packed and down-at-heel, their shutters awry, the paint faded and peeling. Only the pasted-over ROOM VACANT signs evidenced a new lease of life.

There was activity in the avenue—cyclists, pedestrians, honking buses—but the pace was languid, as if in preparation for the heat yet to come. Richard found somewhere to eat within fifty yards. He chose one of several sidewalk tables and ordered eggs and coffee from an incurious colored waiter. It was too early for crowds, though he wasn't entirely alone. Office workers came here—bank clerks, minor officials; their creased suits were as distinctive as uniforms. He ate ravenously while those around him sipped and smoked and read the football results from far-off Europe.

Already it was well past eight. He bought cigarettes himself and left, urgency and a sense of guilt inextricably mingled. Beds of flowers centered the avenue, and at every intersection stone generals and admirals testified to an alien rule. A cruising taxi stopped for him. He spoke no Portuguese and his Spanish was only basic, but it was better than nothing. He produced his Caritas flight pass and with difficulty asked to be taken to local headquarters.

"Red Cross?" the driver suggested after baffled study of the pass. International Red Cross had temporarily suspended mercy flights, but Richard didn't quibble and nodded vigorously. Addresses, contacts, introductions—

he could obtain these. Yet even as they jerked through the gears the sense of impending failure began to form like a hollow in his belly. "What's so special about you? You won't have a chance, father. Not a chance"—in the bright reality of morning the American's unheeded warnings carried a chilling certainty. And in office after office as the day progressed Richard was to find the certainty confirmed.

They were everywhere accessible, everywhere sympathetic, everywhere harassed. Sometimes he was seen straight away, sometimes it meant a restless wait. He left the International Red Cross with a time-saving rag-bag of names and organizations, and one by one he waded through them. There wasn't a field secretary, or his deputy, who didn't greet him during the next few hours or who didn't express concern. But—regrettably—what he proposed was out of the question. Priests, lay-men—no matter who they were, the gist was always the same. The offices changed, the accents and nationalities varied, but not the answers. What Richard envisaged couldn't possibly be mounted at short notice, even if it were practicable. Aircraft limitation, the need for special packaging, the complete absence of any communications link with the affected area—all these must also be taken into account: and so on, and so on. . . . More than once Richard's temper flared. Open hostility might have been easier to bear. To be denied by men and women whose job it was to dispense the aid he sought was devastating. Sweating between appointments in the noonday glare, he tried to summon up new arguments, fresh lines of appeal. But in vain—and his pessimism deepened. Abaguma? . . . There were a dozen Abagu-mas. "Do you imagine, father," one man retorted, matching his own exasperation, "that we don't keep tabs on what's happening on the mainland? Or that, for reasons known only to yourself, we deliberately obstruct the possibility of rescue work? The entire relief effort is an international juggling act. If you think otherwise you're either presumptuous or just plain ignorant."

The understaffed offices were crossroads for journalists

39

and air crews; besieged by those with causes to plead. Richard became increasingly desperate. He pressed harder for attention and argued more passionately when he got it. But he couldn't delude himself forever. Interview by interview, the American was being proved right. At times, in the stifling heat of a cluttered room, he began to find himself hesitating as memories of Abaguma filled his mind and checked the flow of words.

"How will you get back?" a pale, phlegmatic Swede asked as Richard was leaving him. Richard shook his head. The hows and whens of his return were all part of the failure. In black dejection he entered the nearest bar and drank an ice-cold, gaseous beer. As far as trying was concerned, he had reached the end of the road. The names on the Red Cross list were all used up and there was nowhere else to turn. A loaned bed and some given money—these were the sum of what his journey had achieved and they mocked him.

Self-pity didn't enter into it. He drained the glass and stepped out into the burning heat of midafternoon, feeling abysmally lonely and powerless, his spirit crumbling. It had come to this, then.

"Hey, father!" Across the street—Sharkey. The squat figure and twangy voice were unmistakable. "Hey, there—Lawrence!"

Richard raised an arm in tired greeting. Sharkey delayed for a car to pass before hurrying over. "We've been looking for you."

"We?"

"Frank and I. Got some likely sort of information. Made to measure from the sound of it."

"How d'you mean?"

"I'll tell you—but not out in the flaming open." Sharkey gripped his arm and propelled him back into the bar he had just left. "How's it gone?"

"It hasn't."

"Not a bite?"

"What's this about information?"

"Hang on." Sharkey's glance was shrewd. "I'm not going to rush you. Beer, is it? . . . Beer?"

Mystified, Richard nodded. They went to a table and

sat down. The sun scoured the buildings opposite; the shadows were printed like blocks of ink. "Well?"

Sharkey wiped froth from his lips. "I've had word of an aircraft that's lying around doing nothing."

Richard's heart missed a beat, but his tone was flat and disbelieving. "Where?"

"What's more, it's fully loaded."

"Look, if this is a joke—"

"It isn't."

A sight pause, heavy with suspicion. "There's a catch, then."

"No catch. There's a snag—comparatively minor. But no catch."

Whole seconds elapsed this time. "Where is it?"

"Escobar. Ninety miles or so west." A frown made Sharkey explain. "Escobar's one of the neighboring islands."

"What's the snag?"

"The driver's sick. Fever."

"What type of plane?"

"Anson or DC 3—I'm not sure."

"Who's it belong to?"

"Some private setup."

"Private?"

"I didn't get a name, but the facts are okay. Escobar carries an emergency staging strip and the pilot put down there last evening."

The flurry of question and answer ended. Richard remained staring at Sharkey. His shrug had a kind of stunned wryness. "It's too good to be true."

"It's true, all right. Gospel."

"How d'you know?"

"There's a grapevine. And the fellow who told me is one hundred percent reliable."

"What's the plane carrying?"

"You want it all, don't you?—chapter and verse." For a moment Sharkey seemed almost angry. He leaned forward. "It's not arms, if that's what you're thinking."

Nervously Richard lit a cigarette. He dared not hope too much, not again.

41

"Listen," Sharkey said. "Listen to me. Last week a C 46 came into Tomé and was auctioned off to the highest bidder, cargo and all."

"What's that got to do—?"

"This planeload's not so different—motive excepted. Granted it's a genuine relief venture mounted by a private sponsor back in the UK. But it's uncommitted. Don't you get me?—*uncommitted.*" He stabbed the table with a blunt finger. "Aircraft are in demand, father. Someone will want to snaffle this one before you can say knife. So you know what my advice is? If I were you I'd be gone from here faster than snow in July."

Richard ran his hands over his face. They were trembling. "How do you reach Escobar? . . . Ship?"

Sharkey nodded. "Night ferry." He waited, understanding Richard's caution; there had been miscalculation enough. And yet he felt he ought to prod. He liked this man. "What have you got to lose? A wasted journey. But, apart from the chance of a lift back into Uziama, what's to be gained around here?" Richard seemed temporarily to have lost the power of decision, and Sharkey gave him a final push. "Anson or DC 3—either's about perfect for free-dropping. A low stalling speed's essential. You'll never forgive yourself if you don't get over there. It might take the pilot a couple of days to knock the fever out of his system, but when he does that plane could mean manna from heaven."

5

The ferry left at seven. Richard returned with Sharkey to the Rua da Veronica and collected his things. Then, at Sharkey's insistence, they went to a restaurant—"Just," Sharkey said, "to satisfy me that you can and do eat."

Hope had too often been bludgeoned to death, but the Australian's enthusiasm was infectious. Almost despite himself Richard's state of mind shifted. There were imponderables galore and he was careful to guard against overoptimism: everything had been a gamble from the moment he left Abaguma. Yet in one respect he took a more sanguine view than Sharkey, and every time he

42

thought about it he experienced a rising thrill of excitement.

It had been a good many years but, given the chance, he could fly the aircraft himself.

CHAPTER FOUR

1

Richard had his first sight of Escobar in the shadowless gray of early dawn. It was tiny, a volcanic lump shaped like a half-submerged fist. He was practically alone at the rail as the island disclosed its shape and began to take on color. All told there weren't more than a dozen passengers, most of whom were army conscripts, young and sullen and fresh out from home.

The grimy, antiquated steamer must have shaken her rivets loose throughout the ten-hour crossing. Below, the din and heat were unbearable and, along with everybody else, Richard spent the night on deck. Some of the time he managed to sleep, but not to begin with and not after about four in the morning. From then on he waited impatiently for Escobar to show itself. The sky was busy; a number of planes went over. A little before daylight a Constellation droned southward and Richard wondered if it could possibly be Sharkey and Izzard on their way back from Uziama's hazards. "Know something?" Sharkey had said with a thumbs-up farewell at São Tomé's quayside. "You'll have gone a long way around, but you could be cutting all the corners."

Dawn spread like a pink stain and the island turned green; everything was compact and cramped together. A concrete ramp jutted into the waters of a narrow bay and a cluster of houses rimmed the shore. There were no welcoming throngs as the steamer bumped the ramp—only a few locals to make her fast and a slovenly Portuguese sergeant to greet the conscripts.

Richard took his turn at the gangway. The ramp made an elbow-bend in the direction of land. On an impulse Richard risked his Spanish on the waiting sergeant. Was there an aircraft here?—*un aeroplano?* . . . He used his hands. Not military. An aircraft whose pilot was ill, ill since two days ago. *Enfermo,* yes; *si.* . . .

Brown eyes surveyed him without much interest. "A plane?" The intonation wasn't encouraging.

"Yes."

The conscripts were forming up. The sergeant nodded along the ramp. "Ask at the houses," Richard took him to say.

He walked, trailing an elongated shadow. A hut stood at the end of the ramp and he surrendered his sailing ticket to its occupant. There were several houses along the waterfront, a couple of shops, a bar and a handful of fishing boats. Weeds grew between the paving slabs. The timber balcony to one of the houses had collapsed. Apart from an old woman sweeping between the tables outside the bar the place was dead. As Richard approached, the woman called to him in a voice as harsh as a saw on wood.

"D'you speak Spanish?" he asked her.

"Spanish, no." A gap-toothed grin. "But I can understand." Stooped, she hobbled over. "What do you want?"

Richard gazed at the dark, sun-creased face: a more unlikely informant he couldn't imagine and her Portuguese had him guessing. "How far is the airfield?"

"Nothing is far on Escobar."

"How far?"

"Two kilometers."

The conscripts were moving past in a squad, rifles slung, humping their baggage rolls.

"Which way?"

The woman pointed after the soldiers. Then she took Richard completely by surprise. "Is it about the plane?"

"Yes."

"The plane or the fliers?"

Richard's pulse quickened. "Both."

"The plane is at the airfield."

Richard brushed the idiocy aside. "And the fliers?"

"The fliers—the English fliers?"

"That's right."

Nothing much came Escobar's way: São Tomé had the pickings. She expected something and, in his haste, Richard gave her a hundred-escudo note.

"Where are they?"

"One has the fever."

"Yes, but *where?*"

"Here," she said. "They have a room in my house."

Richard was too relieved to feel cheated. "Here?"

"Of course."

"I wish to speak with them."

"You are not the first."

The news jarred, but Richard decided not to press for details; linguistically he was floundering.

"I can speak to them—yes?"

"Of course. Certainly."

She led him into the house next to the bar but had no intention of climbing the stairs. "At the top," was all she said.

"Thank you." He thudded up three at a time. There were two flights. He was halfway up the second when a door opened on the upper landing and a young man stormed out, anger in his voice and glare.

"D'you *have* to make that bloody noise?"

Richard stopped in his tracks. "I'm sorry, very sorry."

"Someone's sick, and it doesn't help—"

"I know, and I'm sorry. I wasn't thinking."

Bare feet, slacks and sweatshirt. "At least you speak English." Twenty, if that. "Who are you, anyway?"

"Look—can I come in? There's a lot I'd like to explain, and—"

"What's wrong with here?"

"It will take some time."

Richard saw the anger and bravado leave the other's eyes; suddenly they were fidgety. "We aren't haggling with anyone."

45

"Who said anything about haggling?"

"There was a fellow last night—"

"Where from?"

"Who cares? He was after the DC 3."

Not an Anson, then. . . . With affected innocence Richard said: "Is that your plane—a Dakota?"

The young man nodded. He was anxious and on the defensive; every minute made it clearer.

"Can I see your friend?"

"He isn't well enough."

"Perhaps I can help in some way. Isn't it possible for me to come in?"

The young man shuffled his feet. "All right. I suppose so."

He was reluctant to the last but stood aside for Richard to enter. The room was almost bare. On one of the two beds an unshaven man sweated and shivered under a covering of blankets. If he was aware of Richard's arrival he didn't show it.

"Have you called a doctor?"

"There isn't one."

Richard moved to the bedside and felt the burning forehead. "Is he like this all the time?"

"It varies. The fever comes and goes."

"When did it start?"

"The evening before last—very suddenly. We were airborne, but he was so bad he couldn't make São Tomé. It only needed another half hour, but he couldn't last out."

"Why didn't you take over?"

"I don't know how—not to make a landing, that is."

Izzard would have winced. . . . A spasm shook the man on the bed. "All in good time," he jerked between clenched teeth. "All in good time, Tony."

Richard said: "If I were you I'd put him on the ferry. He needs more care than you can give him."

"You think so?"

"Isn't it obvious?"

Something rustled in the roof space. Richard glanced about him. There were continents of damp on the flaking

46

walls. He was prepared to go to almost any lengths, but he wasn't lying about the man's condition.

"Who are you?" the younger one repeated in bewildered fashion.

"A priest—Roman Catholic."

"From São Tomé?"

"I'm not a relief official, if that's what you're wondering. I'll explain later. Right now I think you ought to decide about your friend—the steamer leaves in about an hour."

"I—I don't know what to say. Sam's in charge, you see. Sam Dunlop. My name's Goddard, Tony Goddard. It's a long story, but we're from Exeter, in Devon, and—well—with Sam like this the whole thing's at a standstill."

"Who's backing you?"

"Helping Hand."

"Who?"

"Helping Hand. A group of local businessmen thought up the idea, but hundreds of people subscribed to finance us. Sam's a weekend flier, but he's damned good. I've only had a few lessons myself, but I agreed to come along when someone else cried off. We started from Bristol and worked south from there, coast-hopping mainly. Nantes, Oporto, Gibraltar, Agadir, Port-Etienne, Bissau. . . . When we reached São Tomé we were going to place ourselves at the disposal of one of the agencies."

"Which?"

"The one most in need." He gave a disenchanted shrug. Isolation and fevered ramblings had whittled away the crusading zeal and student naïveté. Richard could read him like a book. Just below the surface he was scared. Back in Exeter everything must have seemed very different. "The fellow last night didn't want the cargo—only the plane."

"Gun runner," Richard said.

It didn't seem to sink in. "He was French, I think. Got here by chartered launch. He offered me four thousand pounds."

The man on the bed ground his teeth with sudden frenzy. "Are you putting him on the boat or aren't you?" Richard asked, checking the time.

47

"I suppose I must," Goddard said. "And I suppose I really ought to go with him." He ran his hands distractedly through his hair. "But there's the plane. . . . And if Sam's out of action at all long, God knows what will happen to the cargo. There's a so-called guard at the airstrip, but I don't trust them an inch. And if that cargo goes to waste after all the effort and all people have done and contributed—"

"Don't let it," Richard said, seeing the opening.

"Uh?"

"Fly it out. Put it to use."

"I've told you—I can't."

"Then let me."

"*You?*"

Richard nodded, eyes not leaving Goddard's.

"Fly it, you mean?"

"That's right."

"You said you were a priest."

"So I am. But I used to be in the Air Force. I cut some of me early teeth on Dakotas."

Goddard blinked at him. "As a pilot?"

"Not as a chaplain, I promise you."

Goddard wasn't done with astonishment. He made vaguely incredulous motions with his hands.

"It's like riding a bicycle," Richard said. "Once you've learned you never forget."

"Tail wind," Dunlop chattered, hugging himself blindly on the bed. "Tail wind, Tony. We've got a tail wind."

Goddard flipped his fingers. "What's Sam want with the ferry if you can handle the plane? You really can, can't you? I mean—this isn't some crazy try-on?"

"Not as far as I'm concerned."

Goddard searched Richard's face intently. "How long does the ferry take?"

"Ten hours."

"Well, then—"

"Listen," Richard urged. "There's a lot I haven't told you, and if you wait for me to tell it your friend will miss the steamer. He needs a doctor as soon as—"

"But São Tomé's only half an hour by air. Hell, there's no comparison."

Richard took a deep breath. "I never said anything about flying so São Tomé. That isn't my idea at all."

2

"Where would you fly to then?" It seemed a long time before Goddard got the question out.

"A place called Abaguma. You won't have heard of it, but it's in Biafra."

"But we have to be cleared by São Tomé. We couldn't go direct from here even if we wanted to. Official approval's obligatory. We need an official okay on our destination in Biafra, a code word to insure an unopposed landing—" Goddard broke off, astounded by Richard's ignorance.

"There'd be no landing."

"No landing?" A derisive snort. "Sorry, but I was never any good at riddles."

"We'd off-load your cargo from the air. *Then* we'd head for São Tomé."

Goddard shook his head slowly. "You can't be serious."

"Oh yes. Never more serious in my life."

Dunlop shuddered, teeth clicking a tattoo.

"Abaguma's my parish," Richard said, "and it's starving to death. There's a refugee camp without food and a mission hospital without medical supplies. The district's cut off by road and it hasn't got a landing strip. There's no other way to reach it except by making a series of free-dropping runs, and there's no other plane available except yours. São Tomé's useless as far as Abaguma's concerned. I did the rounds there yesterday and had a bellyful. None of the relief agencies is in a position to cope."

"Helping Hand's committee," Goddard stated uncertainly, "was adamant we kept our noses clean."

"Oh my God," Richard flared. "The dying don't matter, I suppose? What did you come out here for?"

"That's unfair."

"The world's unfair." He glanced quickly at his watch. "D'you want Dunlop on the ferry or not? Take it or leave it. Put him on the steamer and he'll be getting medical attention by this evening."

"You won't fly him?"

"He'll survive," Richard snapped. "But they won't in Abaguma. And unless you get your plane off the ground double quick you'll find it's been picked clean. Either that or the arms boys will be after you again." He paused, banking on Goddard's confusion and insecurity. He was quite blatant about it, without qualms; morality had to take account of intention. "I'll get the plane off for you, and I'll set it down wherever you say—but only if Abaguma comes in between."

"I don't like someone holding a pistol to my head," Goddard countered.

"I've no choice."

"Tail wind." Dunlop jerked. Sweat oiled his face and Goddard wiped it with a wet towel.

"I've no choice," Richard repeated. "It's a matter of life and death. São Tomé would inevitably mean red tape and delay." He swung on his heels in the center of the room. "Don't you recognize a cry for help when you hear one?"

Goddard straightened as if affronted. "I'm as anxious to help as the next man."

"Then do so," Richard said passionately. "For Christ's sake, do so. . . . When you chose to come with Dunlop you did it from the heart, regardless of the consequences, so why not now?"

3

They swaddled Dunlop in blankets and carried him to the steamer. Her cigar-smoking master promised to have a doctor called directly he berthed, and Richard scribbled a brief note requesting its delivery to Sharkey at the Rua da Veronica: *Information correct. Thanks and thanks again. Full story tomorrow when I hope to see you.* It was all done in a hurry, barely ten minutes before departure time, and they didn't wait to watch the steamer nose into the bay. Dunlop was in no condition to be interested in good-byes.

The road to the airstrip twisted inland through undulations of banana clearings. Beyond them the rain forest remained untamed; already it was beginning to quiver as the sun climbed. They soon saw the strip. There were no hangars, no workshops. At its southernmost end a couple of long, tin-roofed huts squatted in the shadows of a colony of palms. Small wonder, Richard reflected, that the conscripts had been surly; someone must have warned them of the silence and solitude in store. And, as though he had read his mind, Goddard suddenly commented: "I was told we were the first to put down here in almost five months."

If he was suffering any misgivings he didn't voice them. Richard thought he seemed relieved to have reached a decision, despite its having been forced on him. As far as the aircraft was concerned, he was very much an amateur, incapable of dealing with Richard's detailed questions. But when he was able to quote Dunlop he was precise enough—with extra fuel tanks built in near the wing roots the plane had a maximum range of 1,700 miles. Two days earlier, with full tanks, they had left the mainland coast at Sassa on what was to have been a five-hundred-mile leg to São Tomé.

"So there's fuel for around twelve hundred?"

"Perhaps a bit more."

Twelve hundred, give or take a few. . . . It was going to be tight; they couldn't risk wandering far.

"What's the cargo consist of?"

"Maize and rice, mainly."

"Bagged?"

"Yes."

"What about medical supplies?"

"They're crated. Also some of the food concentrates."

"Then we'll have to uncrate what we can and pack it in the bags—to cushion the fall," Richard explained. "Free-drop a crate and everything would go to smithereens, even with the ground like a wet sponge."

This was earlier, before Dunlop was put aboard. Now, as they neared the strip, the DC 3 came into view: HELPING HAND was emblazoned in white along the fuselage. To begin with there was no sign of a guard, but several shirt-sleeved soldiers eventually emerged from the huts, the sergeant among them. He spoke to Goddard, who turned to Richard with a look of appeal.

"I think," Richard said, "he's asking about Dunlop."

"Can you tell him?"

"After a fashion."

Richard did his best and the sergeant nodded. Encouraged, Richard fumbled on to say that Goddard and he would fly the plane out later in the day after making certain cargo adjustments. Richard guessed the sergeant understood less than he cared to admit in front of the others, but when Goddard clambered aboard he followed, preceding Richard. It was the cargo that interested him. He fingered the roped stacks of bags, examined the wooden boxes—"Good," he said with envy and without love. "Good." Anything would have been acceptable.

Richard went forward to the cockpit and studied the layout: how long ago was it? A touch of nervousness merged with the sense of elation and he pushed it aside; time enough for nerves. As far as he could recall there were eight or nine control checks—rudder, stick, fuel system, magnetos. . . . But these too could wait. When it came to it he'd remember. He called to Goddard to find something to force the crates and slit the bags. Trimmer, throttles . . . mixture, flaps. . . . An obscene mnemonic came back from the past—harness, hatches. . . . When Goddard returned he had a bayonet plus an outsize needle and twine.

"How on earth—?"

"Sign language," Goddard said. Richard had never seen him smile before: action suited him.

They started on the crates, levering them open. There were ten altogether and it was noon before they were emptied. By then the narrow floor spaces toward the tail were piled with scores of tins and boxes containing a whole range of drugs and vaccines, sterilized dressings and syringes. The heat was almost overpowering; sweat ran from them both in blinding streams. After watching them for a while as if they were lunatics, the sergeant retreated to one of the huts. They went there themselves from time to time to ask for water, singly, never leaving the aircraft unattended, distrust like a sucker on a rose.

The bags weighed about a hundred pounds apiece. They began picking them open as soon as the crates were finished with. Goddard would heave a bag on end and Richard would slit it, shove a number of medical packs deep into the granular contents, then restitch the seam. It would have been exhausting work at any time, but with the sun at its fiercest and the enclosed air thick with dust, they worked and coughed themselves to a standstill.

Around four, stripped to the waist, they lowered themselves to the ground and sprawled gasping in the port wing's shade. The sergeant soon came nosing around again, ostensibly to ask when they intended flying out but in reality to infer that Biafra wasn't the only place in need: to be a soldier on Escobar was almost a punishment.

"I will have to telephone São Tomé," the sergeant said. "They will want to know of your departure."

"We'll go when we've rested," Richard told him. It was hard to be civil; not one of the conscripts had offered or been ordered to lift a finger. He got stiffly to his feet and made some external preflight checks—tires, ailerons, propellers, engine cowlings. If Sharkey's Constellation was old, the Dakota was ancient. After a while he hauled himself back inside and relearned the cockpit drill, memory and instinct merging. Goddard joined him, observing everything he did with a kind of dubious fascination. Goddard's flight charts were penciled and arrowed with sketchy imprecision, the intended stages not always agreeing with where Dunlop had actually put down, question marks and marginal calculations all over the place.

"Have you done *any* navigation?" Richard asked.

"Not really. Sam plotted the tracks." Goddard hesitated; the jargon alone wasn't enough. "I'm very much a passenger, I'm afraid."

"Far from it. But for you the cargo would never get through the door."

Abaguma lay a degree or two east of due north. It wasn't shown on the map, but Richard ringed the district around. "There's a mountain," he explained. "Broken

53

Tooth—very distinctive, with twin peaks. We couldn't have a better marker."

He became edgy as the sun began to discolor the western sky. Dusk would be best for takeoff; darkness followed hard on its heels and would quickly swallow them up. He put it to Goddard, unaware in his single-mindedness how much he had used him, and possibly how badly. Dusk. Half an hour. . . . The consequences could wait. He delayed until the last before letting the sergeant know. As he shrugged into his harness, he prayed above all to be spared rain. Cloud would be bad enough, but rain he dreaded.

He had immediate ignition on both engines and ran them slowly, flicking the magneto switches, adjusting mixture control. Gradually he opened the throttles, watching the instruments react, reacting himself, listening, thinking, remembering. Outside, by the huts, the conscripts pressed hands to their ears. Richard partially shut the throttles down, released the brakes and taxied gently along the strip.

It was still light, but only just. His nerves were taut, yet with the strain there was exhilaration. Butterflies. At the end of the strip he turned and taxied back, growing in confidence, more instinctive, less inclined to snatch. Near the huts he lumbered the Dakota around for the final time and looked at Goddard.

"Okay?"

"Okay."

He crossed himself before sliding the cockpit window to, afraid for a moment, the fear deep and destructive. Then the fear left him and suddenly he was calm. He pushed the throttles forward and the plane's initial surge pressed his spine into the back of the seat. The darkness seemed to thicken as they gathered speed. Acceleration was sluggish and there was tremendous vibration through the undercarriage. Sixty knots, sixty-five. . . . At last he felt the tail come up. Flaps in first position. His eyes were everywhere. Seventy-five, eighty. . . . "Slow but sure"—this from Goddard, hunched trustingly alongside. Ninety. . . . The vibration had lessened. Richard could feel the rushing buoyancy.

Yes, he thought, and when he lifted off he found he did so as if the years between had never existed. The climb was tired and labored but unfaltering, and Richard's heart started to pound his relief.

"*How* long is it?" Goddard called.

"Twelve years." Suez. "No—thirteen."

"What type of plane?"

"Canberra."

Goddard let out a low whistle. They climbed to five thousand feet before Richard leveled. He swung north and coarsened pitch, cruising at one hundred and forty-five knots. It was a fantastic sensation to have the plane respond, to be in control, and he laughed, every scrap of weariness gone.

"Canberras were never this good."

Escobar had vanished within seconds of takeoff. Darkness was already complete and the stars were pricking through. They seemed to appear in groups and the cobalt spread of the sea began to show itself. By Richard's reckoning they wouldn't cross the coast for another hour and twenty minutes. There was no sign of cloud, let alone rain, and he relaxed, thankful, nerves slackening. Abaguma filling his mind's eye. The flat, treeless area in the crook of the stream by the refugee camp was where he must unload. "Manna from heaven"— Sharkey's phrase triggered the memory of another: "Half a miracle will do." And, close to joy, Richard's thoughts congealed around Albert and the sisters and the hundreds who depended on them.

The first they saw of the mainland was the burn-off flares of the oilfield west of Port Harcourt. Immediately, Richard started to lose height. He came down steadily to five hundred feet before leveling out again over the sea. The Dakota bumped and shook on the lower air. Port Harcourt itself was ribboned with light and there were smaller concentrations along the coast. Richard headed in over the Niger's delta, where fingers of water glinted in the cloudless starlight. In the space of the next few minutes he made a number of minor course corrections to take him clear of the Uli run and the possibility

55

of antiaircraft fire. Inland, the Federal-held towns glowed, duplicating their placings on the map, and the rivers also conformed. For sixty or seventy miles nagivation was almost purely visual and couldn't have been easier; even Goddard was in touch.

The battlefront was innocuous enough—a band of blackout and scattered flashes, like flints striking. They were through the danger zone before any mobile battery could possibly have picked them up. Fires dotted the bush as they swept over the enclave. Sometimes a river showed, sometimes a road, sometimes a village—pale and ghostly in the starlight. But the little fires were everywhere, like prayer candles. Ground mist was forming and the forest's undulations grew too close for comfort. Richard climbed. Uli well to port, Uziama diagonally to starboard, neither visible. For a quarter of an hour he continued without deviation. By that time his reckoning told him that Broken Tooth ought to be in view. He searched for it in vain—not for long, though long enough to have him fretting.

"Is that it?" Goddard asked suddenly.

Relief burst in Richard as he saw the split peaks. They were more to the east than he'd supposed. He corrected at once and throttled back a little, excitement hard held.

"Only a few minutes," he told Goddard.

"Shall I open up?"

"Wait awhile."

He went down to a thousand feet, all his newly resurrected skills brought to bear, glimpsing the river and the deserted village where he'd ferried the Land Rover the day before yesterday, swinging left to pick up the stream, cutting his air speed once again.

"Abaguma!"

The word choked his throat. He came in over the town at a hundred and ten knots. Fires where the camp was, lamplight from the hospital. In triumph he swept across the dead-looking township, picturing the faces suddenly turned skyward: amazement would soon replace alarm. He banked, tight with his turn, and started another slow run above the intended dropping patch. It was streaked with mist, but there were no trees and he reckoned he could make a shallow enough approach to flatten out really low before climbing away. Goddard nodded when Richard indicated the refugee camp.

"Across the stream from there—the level stretch. Got it?"

"Got it."

"I'll do a dummy pass to begin with. Start heaving the stuff out when we come over the second time—and mind you don't go with it. I'll make as many runs as you need."

Goddard unclipped his harness and went aft to the door. The Dakota shuddered as Richard spiraled it down and around. It would stall at eighty knots, but he eased the throttle levers back as much as he dared. He made the trial run at what he judged to be about three hundred feet, though the mist made it seem less. He pulled out, sweating, and for Goddard's sake made a less savage turn, wheeling thunderously above the forest.

The hospital was first in line, the town next, then the camp and the dropping area. Every impression was fleeting, but Richard thought he saw someone waving a lantern in the hospital compound. Albert? Sister Marie? Eighty-eight knots and roughly the same height as before. He felt the jerk on the stick and the plane lift as Goddard began shoving the bags out, but he couldn't see what happened to them until he went in on the return run. One had burst open, but the rest—a dozen or so—looked intact; the ground was scored where they'd struck and skidded. Again the stick moved sharply against his grip as Goddard unloaded. Richard climbed, slamming on power. When he came in once more he saw people wading across the stream and he yelled at them uselessly to stay clear. Another stack of bags went hurtling down.

"How's it going?" he shouted, but if Goddard heard he didn't answer: an over-the-shoulder glance showed him working like a madman.

They made eight more runs, each time scattering those who'd reached the area. Richard could imagine the jabber, the excited screaming. There was mercy, after all. He went into a final turn with exultation in his heart and made his alignment on the mission. No shallow dive this time, but in triumph he rocked the wings from side to side as he homed in. The church, the long huts in the fenced compound, his own squat house—for a few brief seconds he had them in view, and among the milling figures there was the one who still swung a lantern.

Goddard had flopped at Richard's side. "Most of the sacks stayed in one piece—all but six or seven."

"I saw."

"They're fighting over them."

"What else did you expect? Queues?" Richard shot Goddard a glance: he had risked so much yet seemed to understand so little. With an intensity of gratitude he added: "You were splendid—thanks."

"How long will the stuff last?"

Richard shrugged. "A few days. All they've been given is reprieve."

"We'll come again?"

"Dunlop and you, I hope. My place is down there." He jerked a thumb. "I can get back via Uziama and mark out the dropping area, lay on some ground aids. It won't often be like tonight. Four times out of five there'll be rain or cloud." He laughed. "They won't much care for us in São Tomé, but we've shown what can be done."

The empty plane had lost its sluggishness: now and again it bobbed like a cork. Richard headed south, skimming toward the battlelines, throttles wide. His elation was such that he was unable to stop talking and Goddard responded, heady with success.

"Sam may not be fit enough for some days yet."

"I'll stand in until he is. From now on *Helping Hand* belongs to Abaguma."

"I'll cable Exeter."

"Despite your dirty nose?"

Goddard grimaced self-consciously. Clusters of fires glowed below, and in a brief reversal of mood Richard thought of all the dead who had died for lack of love and those who would die because of it yet. The frontline blackout came and went. He climbed a shade to spare himself the strain of flying ducks-and-drakes across the forest's roof, growing careless. One and a half hours to journey's end.

"Got a cigarette?" he asked Goddard.

The shells exploded before Goddard could reply. They exploded in rapid succession—wispy flame-centered black-petalled flowers. Evasion was impossible. There were six in the initial clip, though Richard was only aware of three. The first two were ahead, slightly to port, and the Dakota shuddered; the third burst directly underneath and the plane was almost up-ended. In the self-same instant Richard felt a pole-axing kick in the region of his left armpit, followed by a stabbing, razor-sharp pain. As it knifed him into unconsciousness he heard himself shout, "Take her! Take her!" Then for a while there was nothing, no feeling, nothing—as if a door had slammed. Then the raw edges of sensation, like a jagged renewal of life. Then the savage pain swelling high in the shattered arm. He vomited between his thighs, right hand feebly beginning to explore the sticky warmth around the wound.

"Is it bad?"

Vaguely he heard but couldn't answer. The pain came in waves. Air was blowing on his face and the cockpit seemed to be filled with all the din in the world. Down his left side there was blood from shoulder to waist.

"Is it bad?" Goddard was still asking desperately.

Richard vomited again.

"Is it bad?"

"Arm," Richard groaned. "Left arm."

Goddard said: "I won't be able to land. You'll have to do that." Near panic made it sound like a threat. "You'll have to put her down."

Richard nodded. Consciousness ebbed and flowed. There were pulsating moments of numb lucidity during which, with immense effort, he was able to check their height and speed and fuel situation and to correct Goddard's course. And there were periods when the agony of splintered bone and severed nerves clawed him into delirium. He remembered padding the wound with wads of lint from the first-aid box and applying a rough tourniquet, remembered being roused by Goddard and seeing the lights of São Tomé, remembered directing him, remembered taking over, one-handed, and instructing Goddard to slam the throttles back immediately on touchdown.

For as long as he could he kept the obliterating pain at bay, hovering on the fringes of reality. He brought the Dakota in, thudding it onto the runway. Then the spinning thread of awareness began to fray and disintegrate. He clung to it to the last, braking hard, face contorted, but it snapped and was gone before the plane had rolled to a standstill.

BOOK TWO

CHAPTER ONE

1

Howard Lawrence was about to start a beer and sandwich lunch in a pub just off Trafalgar Square when he read about his brother in the midday edition of the *Evening Standard*. PRIEST WOUNDED. . . . UNAUTHORISED BIAFRAN MERCY FLIGHT—the words leaped at him from the page. But no one watching would have noticed the slightest change in his expression. He ate the ham sandwiches, finished the beer, then walked briskly along Whitehall to his office in the Ministry of Defense.

Miss Chancellor, his secretary, was out. He picked up the telephone and asked the operator to get him the British Embassy in Lisbon. The delay was minimal, yet his fingers drummed the desk while he waited for the call to come through.

"Lieutenant-Commander Knipe, please."

There was a crackle, like twigs underfoot. Then the sharp familiar voice: "Knipe, Naval Attaché's department."

"Lawrence here, Theo—Howard Lawrence."

"Howard! Good to hear you."

"I wonder if you'd do something for me?"

"Of course."

"I've just seen a Reuter's report in the *Standard* that's come as a bit of a blow. My brother's been wounded in Biafra, and—"

"Wounded? God, I *am* sorry."

"The by-line's São Tomé. It seems he was shot up while flying over Federal territory. I've no details, but

61

I gather the flight didn't have official approval—something of the kind. Would you do me a favor and find out what sort of state he's in? And another thing—would you pull all the strings you can to have him flown out at the earliest opportunity? He's best away from there if he's in the doghouse."

"What's his name?"

"Richard."

"Who's he with?"

"With? He's a priest."

A surprised pause, a fractional change of inflection. "I'll do all I can. To be honest I never knew you had a brother." Knipe was as clear as if he were in the same building. Crisp and to the point, no waffling about the weather. "I'll call you back as soon as possible."

"Today?"

"I'll try."

"Thanks, Theo."

Howard hung up. The Navy had ways and means of its own, direct lines, contacts where it mattered: Knipe occupied a post he himself had once filled. He unlocked a metal cabinet and took out a batch of files. Most of the signals were classified as RESTRICTED and CONFIDENTIAL, dull stuff, very much routine, but he studied them carefully; trivia sometimes had its uses, cemented gaps.

The telephone buzzed, interrupting him.

"Commander Lawrence, DNI."

"Was that a private call to Lisbon?" the operator asked.

"Yes it was. . . . Sorry." As if she didn't know. His lips curled in derision at a monitoring system that recouped the cost of an overseas call. "Charge me, will you?"

He returned to the signals, but found his thoughts wandering. When he'd lifted the receiver he was half expecting to hear his mother. Afternoon and evening newspapers she abhorred, but Richard might have been mentioned on the BBC news. For the third time in half an hour he spoke to the operator, requesting a Marsden number. "Personal," he added, with a touch of spite.

He lit a cigarette and listened to the ringing tone.

"Tibbie? . . . Howard, Tibbie. Are you behaving yourself, darling?"

"Behaving? Of course." The voice was frail these days—hardly that of a martinet.

"I was thinking of coming down to Wyndhams this evening, darling. Not for long. Just long enough to hear your news and to see how you are."

"When shall I expect you?" Whatever else, she'd obviously neither read nor heard about Richard. "I'll tell Mrs. Wood."

"Don't bother, Tibbie—please. I can't stay," he lied. "There's nothing I'd like more, but I can't, not tonight. I'll come straight from the office and be with you around six thirty."

He returned to the signals. One, from Portland, gave details of the latest ASLD trials. Still in the experimental stage, ASLD was an electronically controlled undersea probe designed to seek out the cold water layers in a submarine's vicinity: beneath such a layer any submarine could hide undetected. Marked TOP SECRET, the signal was too lengthy, too detailed, to be accurately memorized. With overt casualness Howard checked that Miss Chancellor had not returned to the outer office, then took a gilt-edged cigarette case from his pocket and rolled it from left to right across the teletype.

Almost three years ago a podgy-faced man with crinkled hair whom he knew only as Alex had given him this slim, sophisticated camera. In Harrods—"Excuse me, but is this yours? . . ." Actors couldn't have played the scene better. Using a minute light-unit, it photographed with great clarity, even in darkness. It also held eighteen cigarettes and he carried it with him everywhere, relying on the very ordinariness of its appearance, a calculated risk that sometimes woke him in the night as if he'd been challenged.

"I'm a bit late I'm afraid," Miss Chancellor said when she came in. Every afternoon she said virtually the same thing, but Howard made no complaint. What mattered most to him was that she was harmless—harmless because she was uninterested: whoever had recruited her must have had an off day. She was pretty though—straight dark hair, marvelous legs.

"I passed Captain Starey in the corridor and he asked me to ask you if you'd look in on him."

"When?"

"Now, I think."

Geoffrey Starey had a copy of the *Standard* folded on the side of his desk. "Haven't you a brother, Howard? A priest?" He drum-rolled each "r" like Piaf.

Howard nodded. "I've seen the headlines, sir."

Starey looked relieved. "Damned bad luck. I really am most terribly sorry."

"I've been on to Lisbon—Theo Knipe."

Starey cocked an eyebrow. "Oh?"

"Partly in the hope of getting fuller news about Richard, but also to try to lay on whatever assistance he needs. Someone in the embassy will have the ear of the Portuguese authorities concerned."

"Sound move. . . . Is there any way you'd like me to help?"

"I don't think so, thank you, sir."

"It really is a damned shame." Starey's vocabulary was always extraordinarily restricted. As if he realized its inadequacy, he changed tack. "By the way—what did you make of the Portland signal on the latest ASLD trial?"

"Interesting, but not sensational."

Starey was a pocket-tapper when it came to cigarettes. He smoked, but rarely his own; someone usually took the hint. Howard did so now, as he had done a hundred times before, very sure of himself, flicking the cigarette case open. If Starey were ever to suspect anything it wouldn't be the case: he'd been too close to it too often.

"I thought the depth factor well worth further examination," Starey said, finding a lighter.

"I agree." Submarines were Howard's specialty.

Starey seemed to retreat from what he was about to say. "We'll discuss it some other time. You've got other worries." He offered the concerned, oblong smile that was very much his own. "When d'you hope to hear from Knipe?"

"By this evening, all being well."

64

"Have you thought of giving Reuters a try in the meantime?"

"It's an idea," Howard admitted.

He rang Reuters' office as soon as he reached his own. The man at the other end was helpful in the extreme but could tell Howard nothing worthwhile; the piece carried by the *Standard* was taken word for word from the syndicated text, and no fresh information had since come in.

The afternoon dragged. Among Howard's assets was a pigeonhole mind that allowed him to isolate at will. But—unusually—since lunchtime it had failed him. He grew restive, and Knipe kept him waiting until close on five o'clock.

"Howard?"

"Could you speak up a bit?"

"I'm afraid the news isn't too good." At least Knipe didn't beat about the bush. "Your brother's had his left arm amputated."

"Oh, hell."

"I'm told it was antiaircraft fire. . . . I'm also told," Knipe added dubiously, "that he was at the controls at the time."

"It's quite possible. He used to be with the Air Force." Howard paused briefly, dreading the histrionics awaiting him at Wyndhams. "What else?"

"Nothing physical. The operation was this morning and that side of things is as okay as can be expected. But he may be in a spot of bother in other directions."

"Such as?"

"Illegal entry for one. However, don't concern yourself too much. I'm assured the Portuguese will take a sympathetic view because of the background and his being a priest. Another thing is that, as far as I can make out, he was flying a privately financed relief plane without the sponsor's permission. The plane isn't too badly damaged but they aren't likely to feel very charitable toward him."

"What about getting him home?"

"I'm working on that."

"How successfully?"

"Give me a chance, Howard." Sharp little Knipe, one

65

hundred and fifty pounds—if that—wet through. "You could hardly expect him to travel straight away."

"Keep me posted, will you?"

"Naturally. . . . I'm sorry it wasn't better news."

"Thanks all the same. I may not sound it, but I'm very grateful."

2

He told Starey, who made all the appropriate noises. "Does your mother know yet?"

Howard shook his head. "I'm going down there now."

Before leaving he worded a cable to Richard and asked Miss Chancellor to have it dispatched. " 'The Hospital'?" she queried, as if his writing was new to her. "Which hospital?"

"I doubt if there's more than one."

"São Tomé, it is?" She spelled it out.

"Yes."

He was at the door when she said: "And his name's Lawrence too? Father Richard Lawrence—right?"

"He's my brother," he answered.

She presented no threat, but it was as well for her to be informed. Having a brother in the priesthood enhanced the face he presented to the world. The right tie, the right club, the right friends—all helped to protect him from suspicion, allowed him room to maneuver, mitigated against his accepted flaws—a broken marriage, a streak of meanness, a weakness for women.

He took a bus to Waterloo. The train was packed and he had to stand. For fifteen minutes the dreary urban vistas clattered by. After Surbiton they began to break up and by Esher they had largely gone. Sandown racecourse looked a picture; Marsden basked in the warmth of early July. A town suit seemed out of place.

"Good evening, sir." It was amazing how the older drivers remembered. He didn't come too often these days. "What's it like in London?"

"Sticky," he said. "And noisy. And overcrowded."

Wyndhams: only the younger ones needed telling. The house was set well back from the road, as unkempt as the

66

ragged hedge of yews and the sprouting gravel drive. The porch was overgrown with creeper and the door was leprous with flaking paint. Howard pressed the bell, noting the odor of damp, the signs of decay. They seemed worse with every visit. Mrs. Wood eyed him cautiously through a narrow gap before fully opening the door.

"How is she, Mrs. Wood?"

"Quite well, Mr. Howard. Quite chirpy, in fact, since she heard you were coming down."

The smell of must enveloped him as he stepped inside. "And how about you?"

"I can't complain." Her fleeting smile was a contradiction. "None of us can put the clock back."

How she stuck it he couldn't imagine. Ten years of it. No one had lasted more than a month before Mrs. Wood arrived. For two years after his father died housekeepers had come and gone in rapid succession.

"I understand you aren't dining, Mr. Howard."

"That's right," he said.

The stairs creaked. He climbed them slowly, giving himself time. The carpet was worn and the butterflies framed on the landing walls had been there for as long as he could remember: they alone retained their brilliance. He was born in this house; Richard too, four years later. The greater part of what they were had been molded here.

He tapped the bedroom door before entering, licking his lips.

"Howard?"

"Hallo, Tibbie darling." He used the trained expression, the forced kiss. "How's my girl?"

"You're early. You said six thirty."

"I was lucky with the trains."

He pulled a chair against the back of his legs and sat at the bedside. Seventy-one and scarcely a line on her face—selfishness, he reflected, must be good for the skin.

"Mrs. Wood tells me you're positively twinkling today."

"Mrs. Wood always exaggerates."

"But you're well?"

"Well enough," she answered with a touch of defiance. She was propped high on the pillows, shoulders cloaked by a pink-ribboned bed jacket. Silver hair, slim throat, a blue tracing of veins in the bony hands.

"You look gorgeous, darling."

It was second nature to lie and he lied superbly, the cloying approach indistinguishable from sincerity. He talked at random for a while, aiming to soften her, then started uneasily on what had brought him there. "I've some news, Tibbie."

"What kind of news?"

"Not good, darling. It could be worse, a lot worse, but—"

"I don't understand. Is it something to do with you?"

"Richard."

"Richard?"

"He's been wounded, Tibbie."

"I don't believe it." The initial reaction was typical.

"In Biafra. He—he's lost an arm, his left arm."

It came with a rush. Without quite facing her he told her all that he had been told himself. When he finished there was silence. Her lips quivered and her eyes glistened, fever-bright. Then the tears started, the self-centered sobbing, and he deafened himself, staring at the photograph on the bedside table of his dead and dominated father.

3

It had gone eight before he was able to get away. By then she was accusing him—"You should have told me about Richard when you telephoned. Why come all this distance to upset me, then go when I need you?"

"Because," he said gently, but with savagery in his heart, "it was the best way, darling; the kindest way for you. For *you,* Tibbie."

Pity was something he had learned to do without, but it was vital to be liked, to be appreciated. All his life it had been so—before Korea, before the subsequent commitment and the nightmares beneath the controlled calm. To be liked blunted the sense of insecurity.

He was in Hampstead in a fraction over the hour. He turned left down the steep hill from the underground.

His flat was small, in a mansion block. The sober furnishings hinted at a conservative taste, and what was hung on the walls—pictures of submarines once served in, a Dartmouth cadet group, his mention in dispatches—underlined both pride and loyalty.

He lit a cigarette, then went to his desk, so placed as to be invisible from outside, whatever the angle. He opened the cigarette case again, released the hidden catch that lifted the false bottom and took out the spool of film. Held close to the desk lamp, the Portland signal was easily readable under a magnifying glass. One of two incriminating items permanently in the flat was his cipher pad which he kept in the hollow of the bathroom's door handle. This he unscrewed, tore off the pad's top page and returned to the desk to code the signal. In everything he was meticulously careful, wearing gloves, using paper purchased in Woolworth's, making sure his pen left no imprint on the blotter.

The telephone rang. "Howard?" The husky voice was unique.

"Hallo, June."

"I tried earlier but you weren't there."

"I had to go down to Marsden. In fact I only came through the door a few minutes ago."

"How are you placed? Is the day's work done?"

"I wish it were."

"Is that a brush-off?"

"Far from it."

"You couldn't honestly come up?"

"Sorry, June," he said. "I only wish I could." He waited. "No hard feelings?"

She laughed lightly. "You're forgiven."

She was two floors above him, on the fifth. They had met in the lift about six months earlier and she had made it known from the first that she was accessible. Blond, willowy, a solicitor's secretary of all things—she more than anyone was able to ease his tension, dissolve the ferment of his mind.

Howard finished coding the signal, added a request for a routine change of rendezvous, sealed an envelope and slipped it into an inside pocket. Before leaving the flat he burned the spool of film; it was highly inflammable and left only a fine powder which washed away down the kitchen sink. If it hadn't still been light he could have gone to the dead-letter box there and then. Instead he left the flat and took his car from the garage at the rear of the block. There had been times in the past when he had felt himself tailed, once when he had known it, but he had no such feelings now. He drove up the hill to a Spanish restaurant he frequented and he ate alone at a corner table, isolated in his mind too. It was ten before he left and continued with the car as far as the pond. He parked well to the side, then walked down into the dip where a girl giggled in the darkness and a flicked cigarette glowed with the abruptness of a falling star.

The dead-letter box was two hundred yards from the road, at the base of a solitary oak: he could have found it blindfolded. He circled to make certain no one was there then closed in and crouched, dug swiftly with the knife he had brought from the car and unearthed a plain, screw-cap tin. Still using gloves, he transferred the envelope to the tin and the tin to the hole between the oak roots. Three handfuls of soil covered it over, were heeled down and roughened. Then he left, a shadow among shadows, his heartbeat as steady as when he'd arrived.

CHAPTER TWO

1

A weekend intervened before Knipe again came through on the red telephone.

"Something more positive for you, Howard. Your

brother will be saying good-bye to São Tomé next Wednesday."

"Great. . . . Well done."

"He's routed as far as here and I thought I'd better check with you first before arranging his onward move. Reports are that he's in fair enough nick, but he'll be Lisbon-bound on a returning relief plane, which probably won't offer much in the way of comfort. So by the time he arrives with us he could very well want to rest up for a while."

"When does he reach Lisbon—Thursday?"

"Your guess is as good as mine. It's not a scheduled flight. But I wouldn't think Thursday's far wrong."

Howard scribbled down the day and the date. "I'll come out," he decided aloud.

"There's no need, not unless—"

"You've enough on your plate without having to start playing nurse and general secretary."

Knipe chuckled. "As you wish."

"I'll confirm my ETA just as soon as I've got a booking. Would you lay on a car to meet me?"

"Sure."

"Thanks again, Theo."

"I'll pass that on to where it belongs. I'm just the link man."

No sooner had they hung up than Howard dialed Starey on the internal line. Starey's approval was immediate. "How long d'you reckon you'll be away?" he asked.

"It depends very much on Richard's condition, but I can't see myself not being home by Monday." Howard timed his pause to the second. "I've quite a bit of leave in hand, so—"

"I'd forget about leave if I were you. But if your conscience insists on being troublesome I daresay I can find something official for you to do."

"Thank you, sir."

Starey was a cakewalk, always. Half an hour after Howard had told Miss Chancellor to book him on a Lisbon plane that Wednesday evening, she sauntered in and consulted her shorthand.

"Seventeen fifteen from Heathrow, BEA flight number

71

264, arrival time nineteen thirty-five." She looked up as if surprised at her own efficiency. "How will that suit?"

Howard's gaze sheered away from her thighs. There were risks enough as it was. Lancaster had gone that way; Lancaster at Weapons Coordination. "Sounds fine." He nodded.

"I've left the return flight open."

"Fine." He nodded again. "Now—send a personal signal to Lieutenant Commander Theo Knipe at the British Embassy, Lisbon, confirming the flight number and my time of arrival."

"Theo?"

"As in theomorphic." He smiled, concealing the jibe. Miss Chancellor blinked.

"Also request a single-room reservation for me at the Hotel Impala."

"Anything else?"

"Not at the moment."

When she had gone Howard lifted the telephone and asked for Wyndhams. "Tibbie?" He could hardly remember a period during which he'd spoken to her so often: she had made the weekend a special kind of hell. "Tibbie, darling?"

"If it's bad news again, don't go on. Dr. O'Sullivan—"

"It's *not* bad news. I thought you'd like to know that Richard's coming home."

"When?"

"In just a few days. I'm flying out to Lisbon to meet him."

"When?" she demanded.

The pencil snapped in Howard's right hand, but his voice didn't falter. As an enemy she would be impossible.

"On Wednesday—Wednesday evening."

He could picture her with the *Financial Times* spread across her lap. Six days a week it was her morning devotion. Nothing mattered except the state of the market in general and her own shareholdings in particular. An earthquake, a political coup, a hurricane, a war—their sole interest for her was the market's reaction: he could vividly recall how his father, from within the confines of his military mind, had disapproved.

"I want to see Richard as soon as he arrives."

"If it can be arranged, Tibbie—naturally. But you must realize he's bound to need medical treatment and may possibly have to go into hospital."

"If he can travel long distances he can come to visit his mother. That isn't too much to expect of him."

"Of course, Tibbie. Of course."

Damn you, he thought as he said his soft good-byes. He eliminated her ruthlessly from his mind and returned to the waiting stack of files. As usual he looked for the surest indication of being under surveillance—the sudden absence of certain categories of information or an unexplained break in a chain of signals. But there was no cause for alarm. He memorized what was worthwhile and used the cigarette case on details of a proposed change of NATO deployment in the Mediterranean. At five he left the building and went straight home, taking the tube from Charing Cross. The underground breezes were like bad breath. As soon as he reached his flat he confirmed that the single strand of white cotton bridging the gap between bathroom door and lintel remained intact. Next best to surviving unsuspected was to be warned, not taken unawares without a chance of running for cover, and he placed the cotton in position whenever he went out. The price of liberty, he was fond of quoting when the occasion seemed suitable, was eternal vigilance.

The *Daily Telegraph* was where he had left it, the message from his contact a third of the way down the first of the personal columns. Decoded it read: *PQR. Information gratefully received. Arrange fresh personal rendezvous at your discretion. Please notify—Alex.* Howard studied the calendar before drafting a reply. *Suggest rendezvous wooded area to player's right of sixth fairway Burdean Golf Course, Marsden, Thursday, twenty-fourth July, between three and three thirty* P.M. *Delay your confirmation for one week. Am traveling to Lisbon for family reasons. Now follows proposed NATO changes ex Naples. . . .*

He extracted the cipher pad from its hiding place and put the message into code, a code which was never twice the same. Soon after the film spool had been destroyed he drove to the Black Rabbit. Familiar faces, familiar surroundings—they offered a kind of solace: he'd embraced a lonely existence. Toward nine he took the car over to Highgate, where he dined, killing time, waiting for darkness. Dusk was thickening as he left the restaurant and headed along the high road to the top of the Heath.

It still wasn't quite dark enough when he pulled into the curb. He smoked a cigarette and listened to the radio, half envying the couples who strolled by, jealous of the undisciplined carelessness of their lives. He had drunk too much—insufficient to be dangerous, yet enough to soften the rigidity of his mind. Presently he put on his gloves, took the knife and walked down into the saucer-like hollow where the trees were. He had used this dead-letter box for a month. As always when he probed for the tin he wondered if it had been discovered. But it was there, all right. He pried it out, unscrewed the lid and inserted the envelope. A man coughed nearby as Howard was covering the tin and his scalp tightened. For seconds on end he froze, listening, eyes switching from side to side. Then the man coughed again and a girl said, "You smoke too much, that's what." With a tremor of relief Howard finished firming the ground between the exposed tree roots, then walked quickly back to the car.

Whiskey and wine had brought out the hunger in him. He drove home carefully, garaged the car and took the lift to the fifth. A sliver of light showed at the bottom of June's door. Howard checked the time, then pressed the bell.

The door was opened as far as the chain would allow. "Hallo," he said. "Am I still forgiven?"

She studied him, head cocked. "More important, are you drunk?"

"Not quite."

"Not sober, though?"

"Not quite."

Laughing, she slipped the chain and let him in. She was dressed.

Howard said: "I don't give you much warning, do I?"

"There's always a remedy. I could turn you out."

"Get your own back?"

"If you like to put it that way."

"Are you going to?"

"Going to what?"

"Turn me out."

"One of these days, I shouldn't wonder."

"I'm sorry about the other evening."

"You'd hardly say otherwise." She let him kiss her. "Not where you are now." Again. "And how you are now." Her arms were about his neck. "You smell of scotch."

"Policewoman."

"D'you want another?"

He shook his head.

"Coffee?"

"No."

"What, then?"

"Guess."

He led through to the bedroom. She was wearing a yellow trouser suit, black bra and pants. He kicked off his shoes, watching her. Naked, she rolled into the bed and waited for him, her suntan banded white from a bikini.

"Tell me something," she said abstractedly.

"Provided it's respectable."

"The other evening—when I called you."

He stretched beside her and pulled her close. She had the greenest eyes, the most pointed breasts, he'd ever seen.

"What about the other evening?"

"I saw you."

His heart missed a beat, then thudded. "Me? . . . When?"

"After I phoned."

"Me?"

"Yes."

"Nonsense."

"Without a doubt. Up the hill, near the pond."

"You're crazy."

"Not the slightest little bit."

Howard moved his hands, seeking to distract her.

"Crazy. . . . Anyway, what were you doing near the pond at that time of night?"

"At what time of night?"

"Whenever you imagine you saw me."

"Walking," she said. Eyes closed she pressed against him and chuckled huskily. "Walking it off."

"It wasn't me, I can tell you that."

"No?"

"I was downstairs—more's the pity."

"Then all I can say is that you've got a double—an absolute believe-it-or-not double."

Howard covered her mouth with his. No one could be trusted. They might question her one day, following a hunch, a lead. *They.* . . . The worst was always possible. Even talking could be dangerous, so he lay with her and let his body talk for him.

2

The sky was a monochrome gray, but once the Trident pierced the overcast the sunlight was golden. Howard leaned back, his eyes closed against its suddenness, relaxed, temporarily spared the tightrope of his other identity.

Lisbon had filled three years of his life: Naples had followed, then London. Each time his appointed contact had matched the status of his post and the potential of his information. Since Lisbon he had graduated. There was a wide gulf between the glacial suavity of Alex, in London, and the grubby, left-handed Rafael Macerda. In Lisbon, also the methods lacked the slightest finesse. Meetings were always in person, exchanges by word of mouth. Every rendezvous was a gamble. In general Howard had relied on the cinema trick of leaving by a side door halfway through a film and proceeding deviously to whichever café or restaurant had been agreed upon. Although Portugal belonged to NATO, exclusive naval information rarely came Lisbon's way. Yet the risks were greater— often for scraps. And from early on he had despised Macerda, suspecting his dedication, believing him to be a mercenary, paid on results.

All in all it had been a nerve-racking, unproductive period. For a longish while Gillian Shelley had made things a shade more tolerable, but he had wearied of her well before his transfer to Naples; the last few months were a dual pretense.

He yawned. Only the present mattered, the present and the future. Up to now he was clean—tailed for a couple of weeks soon after returning to London, but only for the purposes of a police training exercise; Alex had set his mind at rest on that one. . . . There were wheels within wheels, more than he'd ever know.

They were down on time; immigration and customs were done within minutes. Howard walked through to the hollow-sounding concourse and glanced about him. Knipe's description must have been extra good because he was instantly approached by a dark-uniformed man with a cap-weal across his forehead.

"Commander Lawrence?"

"That's right. Are you—?"

"Green, sir." An embassy identity card was offered for inspection. "Lieutenant Commander Knipe instructed me to meet you." The Yorkshire accent seemed incongruous. "No other luggage, sir?"

"No, nothing except this." A largish briefcase.

"Lieutenant Commander Knipe assumed you'd want to be taken to your hotel. If not, you're welcome at his apartment."

"The hotel, I think," Howard said. "The Impala. It's in the Rua Felipe Folque."

Green pressed his cap on gingerly and guided Howard to the car. "I can see you've been here before, sir."

"Oh yes. Once upon a time."

They headed south, away from the airport, swung right along the Avenida do Basil, then left into the Campo Grande and the Avenida da Republica. Brash new complexes of shops and apartments towered above the baroque and Gothic facades that Howard recalled. But, overall, the changes were relatively superficial. The wide avenues, the downtown monuments and churches, the traffic's impatience, the mellow evening light—all combined to stir Howard's memory. They cruised by the Bossa Nova where, rashly, he and Gillian had once dined; braked near a cinema which he had several times used on his way to meet Macerda. The past was never quite dead, its ghosts never laid.

Green made a couple of right-angle turns in rapid succession before drawing up outside the Impala. "The Lieutenant Commander asked me to give you his private telephone number in case you wish to call him."

"Thanks very much." Howard took the proffered card and got out. "Good night, Green."

"Good night, sir."

The Impala's entrance lobby seemed smaller than he remembered it. He signed the register and was shown to his room. Outside, neon was beginning to pulse and quiver in the purple dusk. He went to the window and looked down into the street, brooding. He had come a long way since he and three others were put ashore north of the thirty-fifth parallel in Korea to investigate the enemy's coastal mining devices. He was a lieutenant then, six years out of Dartmouth, and his capture that night was the turning point of his life. By the time he was released and had returned home he was committed to, and eager to serve, an ideology that would eventually destroy the structure of everything he loathed.

The telephone rang: it was Knipe, as brisk as ever. "Welcome to foreign parts. Green picked you out without trouble?"

"Like a private eye."

"Good flight?"

"Fine, thanks," Howard said. "Once I'd kicked the dust off my shoes I was going to call you to see whether I can persuade you to come and eat with me. Am I too late?"

"Not at all. I'm calling for the same reason, and I insist on being host."

"Nonsense—I'm in your debt already. How soon can you join me?"

"Quarter of an hour?"

"Great."

Howard waited for him downstairs. Their paths had met at Weymouth, years ago, though only briefly. Yet

Howard had no hesitation when Knipe bustled through the doors—the fair hair, the short, slight build, the Cagney-like strut.

"Theo!"

Knipe smiled enthusiastically. "How *are* you, Howard?" He was beginning to thin on top.

"Seeing your tan I feel I've been living under a stone."

"Get yourself a posting in the sun—that's the answer."

"Easier said than done."

They went through to the bar. "What's yours?" Howard asked.

"Gin, please—a pink."

The service was slick. Howard raised his glass. "Cheers —and thanks again for all your help. . . . By the way, is the Miradouro still in business?"

"The *fado* place? Yes, I think so."

"D'you mind going there?"

Knipe's surprise showed. "Of course not."

"Sheer nostalgia," Howard explained. "Absence has made me a tripper."

They walked through the scented streets when the time came: the Miradouro wasn't far. "By the way," Knipe said suddenly as they waited at a crossing, "your brother's arriving about noon tomorrow. *About* is the key word, I'm afraid, but at least we've got an approximation. What time would you like to have the car?"

"Eleven—ten thirty? What d'you say?"

"I'd make it earlier. Ten-ish. Timekeeping isn't exactly a national characteristic."

Howard had somehow forgotten Richard. With a twinge of guilt he asked: "You've no other news, I suppose?"

"Afraid not. . . . But I'm fascinated about what you told me about his once being with the Air Force. When did he quit?"

"After Suez."

"For any special reason?"

"He didn't care for it."

"Politically?"

"He didn't like what war involved."

"How d'you mean?"

"You'd better ask Richard. He makes his own decisions. He's the priest while I'm lapsed and noncontribut-ing, so we don't exactly speak the same language." With measured flippancy Howard finished: "I never saw the light, I'm afraid."

The Miradouro was much as he remembered it—a different decor, all scarlet and white, but otherwise pretty well the same. They drank for a while before asking for a table. The place wasn't crowded; the Lisbon-by-night coach parties would swarm in later.

"Ever here before?" Howard asked Knipe.

"No, I can't say I was."

You bet, Howard thought: the Miradouro was a mec-ca for tourists. Twice, in the men's room, he had kept appointments with Macerda, soft-spoken Macerda who chain-smoked and always stood close, Macerda who came and went in the night and gave nothing in return—no guidance, no gratitude, no confidence.

Two guitarists began to play as Knipe and Howard were shown to a table. While Howard ordered, a middle-aged woman mounted the low dais on which the guitarists sat and began her opening *fado.* It was music that capti-vated him. Over and over in the past he had dined here alone and taken refuge from himself and the strain of his deceits in the plaintive melancholy of such singing. The woman twined a scarf between her fingers and the dark bass notes of the guitar wandered among the com-plexities of the melody.

Knipe made a show of listening. Between songs, How-ard said to him: "Not your cup of tea, I take it?"

"To be honest, no. Hear one and you've heard 'em all."

"You should have told me. We could easily have gone elsewhere."

"Not on your life. For one thing, the food's marvelous."

Iced gazpacho, grilled trout, fruit and coffee. . . . The woman walked off to applause and the conversation picked up.

"Will you be coming out to the embassy?"

Howard shook his head. "I don't think so. I'm only here privately, after all. A lot of water's gone down the Tagus and I wouldn't know anyone now."

"I'm not so sure."

"Who?"

"Geoffrey Shelley." Knipe let it drop like a stone. "How's that for a surprise?"

"Shelley? Still here?"

Knipe nodded. "He was moved for a while—not too sure where, Athens maybe—but they brought him back last year. He's a Portugal man, through and through—language, exceptional local knowledge, everything Lisbon calls for. The powers that be decided he was wasted elsewhere, and in view of his seniority they've upped him to first secretary."

Howard narrowed his eyes. "Shelley was married, wasn't he?"

"Still is."

"What's her name?"

"Gillian."

A flip of the fingers. "Yes, yes—of course."

Knipe gave him a glance that could have meant anything. The crab-red coach loads were beginning to flock in. The guitarists were on their way back to the dais.

"One for the road?" Howard suggested, suddenly insecure. "Lightning's about to strike in the same place twice. For your sake we'd perhaps better go."

Knipe smiled. "I'll cut the one for the road, if it's all the same to you."

"Fair enough." Howard signaled a waiter and asked for his bill. Ten minutes later he and Knipe were outside and Knipe was asking whether he could drop him off at the Impala.

"Kind of you, Theo, but I'll walk."

"More nostalgia?"

Howard shaped his mouth in a grin. "One cognac too many's more like it."

"Green will be with you around ten tomorrow—agreed?"

"Thanks."

"Once you've got your brother in tow and have sized up his condition, call me will you? If there's anything we can do, just ask."

"I will, don't worry."

81

Tires squealed as a taxi U-turned and braked. "Good night then, Howard."

"Good night, and thanks again."

The taxi slid away and was quickly lost in the traffic. Howard didn't wait to watch it go. He walked slowly, deep in thought, with total recall.

"By the way," Gillian Shelley had asked the first time they'd met. "Do you like *fado?*"

CHAPTER THREE

1

Green had him at the airport by twenty past ten, but it had gone one before he heard his name on the public-address system. He was bored with waiting by then, weary of making inquiries. In slightly halting English a female voice requested him to report at the information desk. Howard tossed the magazine he was reading aside and walked impatiently to the center of the concourse.

"I'm Lawrence," he said. "Commander Howard Lawrence." He reckoned they knew by now; he'd been there often enough. "I was told—"

"Ah, Commander Lawrence." Petite and pretty, an olive-skinned girl spiked a sheet of paper. "Your brother has arrived—Father Richard Lawrence, yes?"

"That's him."

"He is in the rest room. I will show you."

She ducked under the counter flap. Unsteady on high heels, hips swaying, she led him out of the public area and along a glistening corridor. A few steps short of the second door she stopped. "He is here," she smiled, motioning Howard forward.

"Obrigado."

He knocked before entering, quite unprepared for what awaited him. Shock held him between strides when he first saw Richard. Sunken-cheeked, sunken-eyed, ragged, unshaven—Howard experienced a long moment of near disbelief.

"Hallo, Richard." Against his will his gaze fastened on the dangling left sleeve.

"Hallo yourself, Howard."

"Don't get up."

"I'm not sitting here forever." Richard pushed himself to his feet. The smile was feeble, the grip weak. "Thanks for coming out."

No one else was in the room. For once—just for once—Howard was moved beyond the inadequacies of speech, yet the words he sought seemed to jam in his throat. He heard himself say lamely: "How's it going?"

"I've been worse."

"You always were an impetuous so-and-so," he began, but it didn't work and he tailed off.

Richard swayed, as if his balance was affected. Howard went to steady him, but Richard pushed him away, shaking his head. "I've got to learn."

"There's a car outside. D'you feel up to walking?"

"Not particularly, but I can."

"It's not far."

"Good." The renewed smile was like an apology. "I'm not normally this groggy, but it's been a bone-shaking trip."

There were two couches in the room, a few chairs, bright prints on the walls—Howard only noticed as they were leaving. The door next along was marked FIRST AID. He glanced sideways at his brother as they walked. Richard's face was a pallid yellow and his eyes moved sluggishly in their dark hollows. Christ, he was thin.

"Who pulled the strings?" Richard asked.

"Someone at the embassy here. Fellow called Knipe."

"Off his own bat?"

"Aided and abetted."

"I'd have been in São Tomé forever otherwise."

"That's what we feared."

83

The sun struck them like a physical blow as they emerged into the open.

"Where are we going?" Richard asked.

"My hotel."

Green was ready with the car. "Good afternoon, sir," he said to Richard, apparently oblivious of the filthy trousers and stained, overlarge bushshirt, blind to the scarecrow appearance and heavy boots. Knipe must have warned him. The doors thudded. He caught Howard's eye in the rearview mirror. "The Impala?"

"Please."

Richard pitched against Howard as Green turned the car. "Sorry." He winced. "They haven't taken the stitches out yet."

"When can that be done?"

"Three to four days."

They said hardly another word until they reached the hotel. Richard had closed his eyes, Howard saw.

"Will you want me again, sir?"

"No thanks, Green. Not today, anyhow."

Howard had already booked a second room, on the same floor as his own. The clerk at the reception desk raised a surprised eyebrow when he saw Richard, but this was his only lapse.

"No baggage?" he inquired after Richard had signed in.

"Not even a toothbrush."

"I'll take him up," Howard said. "Just let me have the key, will you?"

The room was a duplicate of his own. Richard stretched out on the bed. "Sorry again, but would you mind unlacing my boots? There's a knot I can't manage." He joked feebly. "At least I don't wear a tie."

Howard sat at his feet and drew the boots off, dropped them to the floor. "Now, listen," he said, "and tell me if you disagree."

"I'm all ears."

"More than anything I'd say you want to sleep—tomorrow too, most likely. And if that's how you feel I suggest that's what you do. There's no hurry to be moving on. Meanwhile I'm going shopping on your behalf. No self-respecting airline would carry you the way you are now. . . . If you're hungry, call room service. And I'll look in from time to time. . . . Okay?"

"You must have come into money."

"D'you still smoke?"

" 'Fraid so."

Forgetting, Howard said: "Here—catch." He tossed matches and a pack of cigarettes, aiming for Richard's stomach. The matches landed on target but the cigarettes went wide and Richard's left sleeve flapped as the stump jerked.

Howard bent to retrieve the pack and Richard said: "It's odd, you know. I keep believing the arm's still there." He spoke with disinterest, as if it had happened to someone else. "Yesterday, for instance, my wrist was aching."

"What have they given you for it?"

"Nothing a chemist can't provide—Panadol, Veganin, that kind of thing." Richard gazed at the ceiling. "How's Tibbie?"

"She sent her love and wants to see you at the earliest opportunity. Insists, in fact. Commands."

"What about her health?"

"She wouldn't like you to think it's better."

Richard turned his head. Without reproof, he said: "You haven't changed, I see. . . . What about Jessica?"

"What about her?" Howard replied, defensively.

"How is she?"

"Well."

"And the kids?"

"Fine."

"Have you seen them recently?"

Howard held his tongue. *Don't start on that,* his mind snapped. *Not now. Not so soon. A man's wife and children are his own affair.* . . . He stared uncertainly at his brother, shabby servant of a nonexistent God, maimed in the cause of nursery-rhyme beliefs. It was the wrong century for superstition.

"D'you know your trouble?" he said, making it comic.

"Tell me."

"You look at life through stained-glass windows."

"You once did the same."

Howard nodded. "And didn't like the view."

The rumble of traffic reached them from the street below.

"Is the view any better now?"

Howard wasn't to be drawn. He shrugged and laughed, moving to the door. "No need to waste your sympathy on me."

"Sympathy's never wasted."

God, Howard thought, *how bloody smug you've become.*

2

The dream immersed him during the night, the self-same dream that came to hound him time and again, leaving him wide-eyed and sweating. It was the dream of a blind man, all voices and sensation, darkness everywhere, nothing and no one to be seen. First his parents in argument, his mother's tongue at its sharpest, wearing his father down until he no longer answered, let alone struck back—"It was my dearest wish that they follow you into the Army. You knew it, yet you never once took my side or attempted to influence them. . . . *Never.*" Then his father in the enclosed space of the confessional, dutifully listing his sins of omission. Even in the dream Howard was aware it was a dream. He listened to himself shouting: "It wasn't your fault. You did nothing wrong. We chose as we did because of her. Because of *her.* . . . We were stronger than you."

A hollow was in his stomach, a sense of loss. Clichés from the pulpit, the sound of a newspaper being opened and turned, his mother's voice again, telephoning—"This massacre in the papers today, George—what do you advise? Should I hold or sell?" Resentment filled his emptiness. In the sweatbox now, separated from the others who were captured with him, a quiet voice close to his ear: "Don't you see? Don't you see? You could help. Everyone—yes, everyone. In time."

Unknown to him he twisted on the bed, grinding his teeth. Jessica was there, very clear: "Who *are* you, for God's sake? After eight years I'm beginning to think I married a chameleon." It was from life, that; she'd actually said it. And then he was running, slowly at first but with increasing speed, running from everything he knew, faster and faster, until suddenly he jerked into consciousness, propped stiffly on his elbows, panting and feeling the cold leaking sweat.

Time and again it had happened, wits frantically resurrecting. And this time he was in the Impala. In Lisbon. And Richard had arrived. And Shelley was back in the embassy. And the Burdean rendezvous with Alex was a week away.

Yes. Yes. . . .

He left Richard alone until midmorning. When he finally knocked at his door he was surprised to find him already dressed.

"Not bad," Howard exclaimed, eyeing him. Black suit, slip-on shoes, white cotton roll-neck—the suit hung loosely, but the rest seemed to fit. They were of identical height and, normally, much the same build. "How long's that taken you?"

Richard smiled. "About three hours. Buttons are the main trouble."

"Why so early, though?"

"There's nothing much to be gained by lying around."

"I don't know a doctor who'd agree with you—not so soon."

"I'd rather get on home," Richard said.

"I told you last night—there's no hurry. Not as far as I'm concerned.

Richard didn't seem to hear. "Could we make it tomorrow?"

"If that's what you really want. . . . I'll do my best—if not tomorrow, the next day."

"Are you still in Hampstead?"

Howard nodded. With reluctance he said: "You're welcome there."

"Thanks, but I'll go to Wyndhams."

"She'll drive you mad, you know. Up the wall." Howard expected a comment, but none was forthcoming. "How long have you been away? Two years, is it?"

"Two and a bit."

The empty sleeve inhibited Howard. He sat on the edge of the bed, reserve in his glance, restraint upon his mouth, imprisoned by his own state of mind. He had scarcely questioned Richard about Biafra. He found it difficult. The greater part of him was unconcerned with the dilemmas and desperations of other people, and what remained was ill at ease with those who were.

"Are you going to be in trouble as a result of what you did? With your bishop and so on?"

"Very likely."

"What will happen?"

"I honestly don't know. And I'd rather not talk about it."

"Okay." Howard rose. "How about getting yourself an English paper or two and sitting somewhere in the sun while I make the flight bookings? Once that's done we could lunch somewhere then come back to the hotel and make the most of siesta time. What d'you say?"

He hadn't money enough to buy a ticket for Richard, so he telephoned Knipe asking for help.

"Richard's foreign currency allowance hasn't been touched. Can I have the fare charged to the embassy, then get him to settle when he's back home and more fully recovered?"

"I suppose so. I'll find out. . . . Has he a passport?—I forget."

"As good as—temporary papers. They'll see him safely into the UK."

"None of this is really my line," Knipe said crisply, as if to stress his merits, "but I'll chase it up. Meanwhile, if I were you, I'd go ahead. By the way—"

"Yes?"

"Geoffrey Shelley sends his best wishes."

Inevitably the clerk at the travel agency checked with the embassy before issuing a ticket for Richard, but there was no hanging about; Knipe was certainly a mover. Howard chose the following afternoon's Trident, due at Heathrow at sixteen fifty-five. Then he collected his brother and they went by taxi to a restaurant near the

88

Rossio, where the thronged black-and-white patterned pavements were as colorful as a crowd scene in a musical, at once animated and nonchalant.

"Hungry?" Howard asked.

"Not very."

"Which would you prefer—inside or out."

"Out, I think."

An umbrella shaded them. A blind singer plucked his guitar across the street and the salty tang of the Tagus freshened the hot air. Howard ordered for them both—a main course and a carafe of wine. He would have pulled Richard's leg about it being Friday, malice behind the good humor, but he let the chance go. They were more like acquaintants than brothers. In any case it was too early for taunts; too early, it sometimes seemed, for any conversation at all.

Howard broke a particularly long pause: "Which papers did you get?"

"*Times* and *Mail*."

"Anything worthwhile?"

"A paragraph or two."

"About?"

"A Mig raid on Uruta. Sixty killed, a hundred wounded. It rates a few lines, I suppose."

Howard had never heard him so bitter. They finished eating and his eyes called a waiter, asking for coffee. He gazed at the mainly masculine crowds. Sandwiched between a dozen thoughts, he wondered what had become of Macerda and whether he was still in business; it had been business for him, a living. They had worked the direct link system, one to another, and it had its advantages; there was no cell, no network, at risk. Only oneself and at most two others could be squandered.

He raised his cup to his lips. "I used to come here in the old days," he said to Richard out of the blue, a gentleness in the voice that was at odds with the sharpness of the eyes. He offered Richard a cigarette and took one himself, lit them both and poured smoke from his nostrils, the fragrant smoke he would always associate with Lisbon.

A ragged man limped to his side, offering a shoe shine, and he waved him away.

"He can do mine," Richard said.

"Yours? But they're new. Dammit, I only bought them yesterday."

"Even so." Richard signaled to the man, who hurriedly placed the wooden block in position and knelt in front of him.

"But they're new," Howard protested forcibly. "Brand, bloody new."

"And the man's hungry—just look at him. Which is more important?"

"Don't preach," Howard warned, with a surge of anger that defeated all he'd promised himself.

He glared at the passing crowds. People existed to provide an opportunity for power—somehow he managed to control the inner turbulence and not to say that too. He could never openly be his true self. It was part of his own penance, as demanding as his brother's celibacy.

3

In the morning Howard thanked Knipe for all his assistance and was rewarded by having Green arrive with the CD-plated car. While they waited at the airport for their flight to be called, Richard scanned the newspapers, spreading them across his knees, shoulder stump jerking involuntarily as he sought to control the pages. He wasn't quite so haggard, but only for brief moments did his strained face soften, the mouth loosen, the muscles in the jaws unclench. And he still tottered occasionally, seeking his center of gravity. As he entered the aircraft door he tripped and nearly fell.

Whatever else, Howard couldn't help but admire his courage. He himself had been spared much pain. Only once had he suffered its deliberate application—and then not for long. His Korean guards had shoved him into the sweatbox to show the others that he wasn't exempt from punishment. But it was play-acting, a deceit, the first of innumerable deceits. Before he ever stepped ashore with the landing party he was already a potential accomplice, disenchanted by the conventions of a wornout faith and the growing corruption of an effete society, anxious to be what he was—even if it meant that friends and colleagues must continue to assume that he was someone else.

Lisbon had fallen away. There were no clouds. Portugal, then northwest Spain, then the Bay, then Brittany— in turn they spread beneath them like a map. Richard slept for about an hour. The stewardesses came and went, their hips brushing Howard's shoulder. He bought whiskey and cigarettes for Richard as well as for himself, using his last escudos and paying the balance in sterling, a remark he passed making the girl laugh and shake her head. He could lose himself in a woman, even momentarily.

London shared the same cloudless sky and brilliant sunshine. Howard dialed the Wyndhams number from Heathrow. "Mrs. Wood?"

"Yes? . . . Oh, it's you, Mr. Howard."

"My brother and I are at the airport and we'll be coming down to Wyndhams almost straight away. Would you please let Mrs. Lawrence know? And another thing— we'll both be staying."

"Very well, Mr. Howard. Mrs. Lawrence *will* be excited, really thrilled, when I tell her. She's worried so about Mr. Richard."

Balls, he thought.

"How is he?"

"Better than I'd expected. Not too bad, considering."

Marsden was a stone's throw—ten miles, at most, and the taxi driver knew the shortcuts: dead on a quarter to six the tires were crunching on the half-moon drive. Howard saw Richard look in astonishment at the choked flower beds, the unweeded gravel, the Virginia creeper that bulged in profusion across the front of the house.

"Doesn't Taplow come any more?"

"Once a week, I believe."

"Surely it used to be every other day?"

Howard nodded. "What she can see from her bedroom is all that matters—the rest can go hang. It's in character."

Mrs. Wood opened the door, pink in the face with emotion. "Mr. Richard!" she exclaimed. "Welcome home, Mr. Richard."

"Hallo, Mrs. Wood. Good to see you. What's more,

you haven't changed a scrap, not a scrap. How's the lumbago?"

She used her stock phrase. "I can't complain." Perhaps his appearance restrained her. "We're having a magnificent summer—Mr. Howard has probably told you—and I think the warm weather helps."

Howard followed Richard into the gloomy hall with its awful wallpaper and tired paint. "Where are you putting us, Mrs. Wood?"

"At the end of the landing. The rooms are nowhere near ready yet, but—"

"I only want to dump my case on the way."

They had hardly reached the landing when they heard Tibbie calling, her voice as demanding as a fractious child's—"Is that you, Richard? Is that you?" Howard's mouth tightened. Home was a word, a house, an address, a kind of museum. Was it the same for Richard? He often wondered but didn't know. For years they had remained at arm's length. Once it was otherwise, but that was long ago: the past was a foreign country.

Tibbie's gaze was not for him as they entered. "Richard." Her thin, sinewy arms widened like a grab. "Richard. . . ." The tears came welling up from her armory. "Poor boy, poor boy."

"Hallo, mother."

Howard crossed to the window and stared out on the immaculate patch that Taplow maintained amid the wilderness—the corner of lawn, the rock garden, the roses.

"What came over you, Richard? What made you do it? Why didn't you refuse? Look at you, just look at you. . . ."

How vague she was. Howard turned impatiently. Quiet-voiced, Richard withdrew from Tibbie's grasp. "What I did was my own fault." He smiled. *"Mea culpa,* mother."

The Latin she understood, and the context from which it came. Sundays and holy days, year in, year out, she had mouthed responses, knelt and sat and listened. But faith itself was a language she had never learned. Charity was a coin in the plate, self-sacrifice a check in the post. To give anything of oneself was incomprehensible stupidity.

"I don't follow you," she was saying to Richard.

"It was just bad luck. It could have happened to anyone."

"Then how was it your fault?" Already the tears had ceased, the jaw was jutting.

"What I mean is that no one's to blame, no one except myself. It's a long story, but—well—the pilot of that particular plane was sick and I took over from him."

"Why?" she insisted. "You finished with airplanes when you made up your mind—"

"There wasn't anyone else."

"Couldn't you have waited?"

With controlled passion Richard said: "They were starving, mother. Starving to death. Surely you've heard how bad it is?"

Richard talked on, gently, persuasively—mentioning names and places, describing scenes, explaining reasons, and she quietened, unheeding, waiting for him to finish. With bad grace Howard marveled at Richard's patience. Equally, he envied his capacity to handle her. No flattery—nothing like that. He moved from the window, unwilling to listen any more, unwilling to stay and remain ignored. There was coldness in him, pique. Once in a while he recognized this facet of himself.

He said: "You'll never win, Tibbie darling, so don't try. Richard always argues out of the top of his heart—remember? And he keeps God in reserve to have the last word."

She laughed absently, a brittle little laugh that somehow emphasized how frail she was. Howard crossed to the door, pausing before he let himself out.

"Shall I get Mrs. Wood to bring you your brandy soda?"

"Please." She didn't turn her head.

He lit a cigarette on the stairs, then went into the garden by way of the kitchen. Half an hour passed before Richard joined him, during which time he paced back and forth, back and forth, thinking of Alex and the fragments he gave him, the fragments out of which an overall pattern could often be formed, a technique pieced together, an estimate made. There was consolation in achievement, reward in Alex's commendations. But here there was nothing and never had been—unless he counted his father's rare, disheartening praise.

He was heeling out the cigarette when he saw Richard coming. Deadpan, he said: "I notice you haven't lost the bedside manner."

Richard didn't rise to it. "What d'you make of her?"

"As well as can be expected, I think the phrase is. But you're the one who's been away. You'd notice any change."

"I do, and its for the worse. How often d'you come down?"

"Once, twice, a month. It depends."

"What does O'Sullivan say?"

"I only know what Tibbie says he says, which is no guide at all."

They kicked through the long grass, Richard grasping the stump of his arm as if it ached. "Wasn't this the croquet lawn?"

"Way back."

They stopped, looking about them at the high tangles of laurel and rhododendron, the grass-choked broom, the untended azaleas. The sickly-sweet smell of lime tree blossom filled the air.

"It wasn't too bad when I was last here," Richard said. "When did the rot set in?"

"Say a couple of years ago. But it's been steadily going to rack and ruin for longer than that—the house as well. Surely you'd noticed?"

"I suppose so."

"If I cared," Howard said, "I would weep."

"And you don't care?"

"No."

"Not at all?"

"Not a brass farthing." The clatter of a mower reached them from the edge of earshot. "Why should I? Why should you, for that matter? We hated the place when we were younger, both of us, and you know it. What's happened since to make us change our minds? We've hardly lived here. Only duty brings us back."

Richard said nothing.

"Sorry, I forgot—you'd never admit to that even if

you agreed." The sarcasm was less telling than usual. "But if you claim that Wyndhams retains some remembered magic, or whatever, I'll call you a liar to your face. It was a stinking place to be young in. All those rows, the endless domineering—Christ! If only he'd stood up to her. If only he'd so much as tried to get the whip hand. . . ."

Howard's voice trembled, vibrant with contempt and longing. He was safe with Richard, as safe as it was possible to be safe. Richard was the only one to whom he could pour out the lava-flow of his hatred: it had festered in his absence. He listened to himself, wary even now, going as far as he dared.

"If there's one place I'm pleased to see rot, this is it. It may have looked better then, but it wasn't, not for us, not in the ways that mattered. You and I owe it nothing. We were in rebellion as soon as we knew the meaning of the word."

Richard stumbled slightly, grimacing as the pain jarred in the upper arm, but Howard didn't notice. At some untraceable point within himself he despaired, afraid for a moment of what he was, seeking an excuse, a justification, as if he'd suddenly been found out.

"D'you remember Austria? . . . Steyrhofen?"

Richard frowned. "Of course." The deep snow and the tiny village. Years ago.

"I often think of it. It was the first time you and I were away without them, the best time we ever shared." Howard plucked a fistful of long grass. "No public humiliations, no bloody talk about money, no being ashamed of belonging to them—"

"That's going too far," Richard protested.

"Is it?" He scowled at Tibbie's window. "I remember your once saying that all Wyndhams meant for you was rain and tears."

Richard faced him, arm still slung across his chest. "What's got into you? Why so sour?"

"I don't like this place."

"You've made that pretty obvious." A puzzled, searching stare that lasted. "Is there some other trouble?"

"Nothing." Howard was quick, perhaps too quick. He

was instantly on the retreat, covering up. "I haven't blown my top in a couple of years. There hasn't been an opportunity. It isn't something I can do with anyone else."

"But what are you blowing your top about, for God's sake? The past or the present? What's so wrong with the present where you're concerned? It seems to me you've got the kind of life you want."

Howard shrugged the questions away, unwilling to debate.

"You distort everything so much," Richard said. "Go on like that and it could warp you." He turned and made for the house. His tone changed. "I'll see O'Sullivan on Monday about my stitches and ask him how Tibbie is. She's withered. There's a waxy look about her; haven't you noticed?" Howard came alongside and Richard said: "Don't let the past haunt you. I don't mean to preach, but what's done is done. Show her a little affection. She needs that more than anything."

Howard could not quite let go. "We did once."

"I'm talking about now."

CHAPTER FOUR

1

He returned to Hampstead on the Sunday night, Whitehall on Monday morning. Miss Chancellor hadn't arrived, but Starey was his usual stolid self.

"Wondered whether you'd be here. How did everything go?"

"Like clockwork, thanks to Knipe."

"How's your brother?"

"Worn out and as thin as a rake, but surprisingly resilient. He must be as tough as old boots."

"Good, good. I'm glad." Starey tested the smoothness of his chin. "Lisbon and I were in touch at the end of the week. I gather you kept clear of the embassy?"

"Yes, I did."

"You ought to have looked in, you know. As a courtesy."

"In view of the fact that I was in Lisbon in a private capacity I thought—"

"Even so," Starey interrupted, ending it there. "However, no harm done—and I'm relieved about your brother."

The unexpected reprimands were the ones that stung. Howard retreated along the corridor, face burning. Miss Chancellor was languidly removing the typewriter cover when he reached his office: he snapped at her for being late and she blinked back as if she couldn't believe her ears.

There was nothing in the *Daily Telegraph* for him. He knew there wouldn't be; it was too early. Yet for the second time that morning he checked the personal columns.

"Is this all?" he asked Miss Chancellor when she brought him the day's files. "What about the signals while I was away?"

She flounced off indignantly: two could play at *that* game, her walk said. She returned a few minutes later and thudded a stack of folders on his desk. Two worlds were overlapping as he started to wade through them, one of which offered a kind of revenge, placated a need that smoldered and sought fulfillment. Where and how it would end he didn't know and was sometimes afraid to think. He had outlawed himself. There were times when, mellow with drink and relaxed with a woman, he could dismiss his fears. All would be well. He was a willing convert, a volunteer with years of proven, unspectacular service. There would be no blackmail if, through circumstances, he failed to deliver or he outlived his usefulness. He had been assured of it, promised a haven, a place to go. Alex had given the assurance in the semidarkness

97

of a Soho strip club, whispering while others watched.
. . . But optimism wasn't always in control. Early morning
and alone—there was often no confidence then. He would
search around his brain for the conviction he needed, re-
analyzing the sincerity of Alex's glass-smooth voice—
"But of course. Of course. Don't worry about such things.
. . . You will be looked after." They owed him something, he would tell himself. London, Naples, Lisbon—
each had helped him to make a worthwhile contribution;
and before Lisbon, while he was still an active sub-
mariner, he had used what opportunities there were. It
would count in his favor, surely? It must.

His mind was free of all this as the day passed. On
his way to lunch a placard caught his eye—OIL AND
NIGERIA: THE STAKES ARE HIGH—and he wondered how
Richard would have reacted. "You see?" he wished to
say, imagining him present. "The world isn't the way you
want it and never will be. You're kidding yourself if you
believe otherwise. You're out of date. Everything you
stand for is out of date. It hasn't the power to change
anything anymore."

An interdepartmental committee meeting took up
most of the afternoon. The room was like a hothouse
and everyone bickered and yawned and smoked too
much. Howard was glad to escape and fight his way
home on the tube; at least it was cooler below.

The cotton on the bathroom door was unbroken, as
it was on his return from Lisbon. He showered and
changed, then rang June.

"Where've you been?" she asked. "Where on earth—?"

"Away."

"Very funny."

"Lisbon," he admitted.

"I must be in the wrong business." She sighed. "I
don't know, everyone goes where I want to go except
me."

"I went to collect my brother."

"I've heard stranger explanations, but none so unbe-
lievable. 'Collect,' indeed."

"I'll explain in more detail later."

"Later?"

"That was my idea."

"How much later?"

"I thought we might eat up the hill. Chinese, if you like."

"How will I know you won't be your spitting-image double?"

It caught him off guard and he very nearly faltered. "I'll be wearing brown hobnailed boots. . . . Knock on your way down, will you?" His lips were curled and a vein corded his forehead below the hairline. With a kind of self-mockery he said: "Did you miss me?"

"Miss you? I damn near kicked your door in."

She hung up, laughing. He caught sight of his face in the mirror beside the Dartmouth photograph and stared at what was written there in lines and shadows as if he were scrutinizing something else.

Another photograph was nearby, a snapshot, and in it he lay spread-eagled on snow, grinning like a maniac, skis crossed, pointing a stick defiantly at the camera: Richard had taken it at Steyrhofen, and Howard never failed to be reminded of the glittering beauty and great peacefulness of the snow. It had seemed to isolate Steyrhofen from the rest of the world, and in that isolation he had found a happiness that went far beyond the gaiety and attachments of *après* ski and the joyous indignities of the nursery slopes. The snow that blanketed the village and the swelling hillsides was everywhere crisp and pure, and it had somehow conveyed to him an enormous sense of security.

Korea was yet to come, a thousand uncertainties were yet unborn, but insecurity was nothing new and for three weeks he'd been free of it, close to Richard, closer than at any time—Richard who had also reveled in the feeling of refuge and who, on the last day of their leave, before riding down in the cable car for the final time, had jokingly said to him and the girls they were with: "We don't *have* to go home, do we? I mean, we've choices open to us. For instance, all those in favor of defecting Eastward please raise their right hand—now!"

Everyone's hand had gone up. Nothing had been serious at Steyrhofen.

Howard looked at the snapshot and then at the reflection of himself again: they were different faces, and time alone was not responsible.

2

It was Wednesday before the *Daily Telegraph* had anything for him. The moment he heard the paper being pushed through the letter box he was rolling out of bed. The message filled two lines and began with the figure 17, the cipher page number: broken down it was even more curt—*PQR. Agree sixth fairway Burdean Golf Course tomorrow and time—Alex.*

Relieved, Howard went about his day. Loneliness took many forms, had many allies, and he had come to know them all. Desertion was the one he perhaps feared most. Two or three months sometimes elapsed without personal contact with Alex, and weeks could pass before a coded exchange was made. He would suffer if ever the gap was overlong, frightened in his guts lest he had been abandoned, manufacturing reasons why and why not, drinking too much as the days dragged on. "You will be looked after"—why doubt after that? Why be afraid? He had harangued himself about this and his lack of faith, yet no sooner had a couple of blank weeks gone by than his nerves were as destructive as ever.

He would have preferred to take a day's leave, but he wasn't going to ask Starey another favor; not so soon. He would also have preferred the rendezvous to be at the weekend, but had chosen Thursday because the course would be less crowded. He had no intention of visiting Wyndhams; it was hardly the time to set off from the house for a round of golf—or to call in afterward. Starey could assume what he liked. Starey was a pushover, anyway; until Monday he had never so much as hinted that Howard had put a foot wrong.

He ate in town that evening, then returned to his flat. Alex's English was good, but he preferred not to memorize: a report was expected. Typed, Howard's made three quarto pages, combining photographed fact with summarized policy determinations and substantiated gossip. It took time, but the long July dusk was still in possession when he left the flat and went down to the garage: he kept his golf clubs there. He shut himself in and took a 4-iron from the bag. The hollow shaft was an emergency cache for his cipher pad, one of several places kept in reserve, but it was equally suitable for a slim roll of quarto. He uncapped the end of the club and inserted his report. Minutes later the club was back in the bag and the bag was locked in the trunk of his car and he was riding up in the lift, ready for a final whiskey before going to bed.

There were no dreams. He woke too early; it was always the same when he was about to meet Alex. The sun was pushing low, level rays into his bedroom, promising another glittering day. He lay there for a while, as near to being relaxed as he knew it to mean, thinking back, thinking forward. Alex was his mainstay. Their greetings might be sketchy, their conversations within close limits, yet Howard sensed friendship. It was a rare feeling and he had a longing for it. He'd been a loner for more years than he could recall. "You ought to have more friends," his father sometimes used to remark in a tone of wistful complaint. "Friends are a measure of what you're giving to life. You'll need 'em one day, mark my words. I'm not talking about acquaintances—they're ten a penny. Friends are rare."

Howard made a long arm for a cigarette and switched on the radio. Alex was rare. He was no mere go-between. There was nothing furtive in his manner, nothing degrading in the way that contact with Macerda had been degrading. Sometimes he didn't quite look at you and sometimes his smile wasn't quite a smile, but these were trifles. On days when a meeting was imminent the nightmare of the connection between them being severed was unimaginable.

He left the flat at noon with time to kill and took the route that suited him best. He pub-lunched in Richmond before heading for Walton. Traffic was light, but mainly he kept to the slow lane. A change was coming over the day. Huge cauliflower heads of cloud were piling to the south and the air was heavy; just short of Walton a warning flurry of rain beat at the windscreen. A sign post pointed to Marsden, jolting Howard's mind to where it least wanted to go—he'd forgotten to call Richard to hear what O'Sullivan had had to say about Tibbie. Christ, he thought, pushing through the gears at Walton Bridge. Christ, he'd promised. . . . Well, it would have to wait until tonight. It would look bad, but he'd think of something. Excuses were his stock-in-trade.

He went the long way around to Burdean, completely avoiding Marsden and never coming nearer to Wyndhams than about a mile. It was a little after two when he made the right-hand turn to the clubhouse. Only three cars were in the park as he unlocked the trunk and took out his bag. On his way to the locker room he was struck by a few stinging blobs of rain, as heavy as bird droppings.

Brogan, the resident professional, called to him as he passed the shop: "You're a braver man than I am, sir."

"It might pass over."

"Not on your life."

Howard squinted at the sky, then grinned. "I need the exercise, you don't."

He played off twelve. Burdean asked all that of him and usually more: it was no place for beginners. The fairways were narrow and undulating, enclosed by gorse and pines. Angles were everywhere deceptive, accuracy paramount. The first hole was a longish dogleg, the second an immensely testing 485 yards, the third a tricky 5-iron to a heavily bunkered green. Howard kept a close eye on his watch. The atmosphere was leaden; the gorse and pines stood motionless and the thunderheads were pewter-colored against the sky's deepening blue. As he chipped up to the fourth another teasing shower pelted him. He wiped his face and played on. Far to the right, in a gap between the pines and across two fairways he saw a couple hurrying to finish the eighteenth; whatever else, they'd be home and dry. Five minutes to three. . . . He made a mess of the fifth, thoughts elsewhere, overrunning the green and three-putting. It was of no consequence. Pacing himself was all-important; Alex liked punctuality.

At ten past three he stood on the raised sixth tee, facing another dogleg. The fairway narrowed at around 180 yards, waisting in, a thick wedge of pines protruding from the right. Howard studied the area intensely, but there was no sign of Alex; a platoon could have been in hiding. He took a 3-iron and deliberately sliced his ball into the trees. With satisfaction he watched it disappear from view, played a second ball straight and slightly short, changed to the club he required, then headed with his trolley for where Alex waited.

He had been among the pines for a full minute before a low whistle gave him a lead. Even then Alex wasn't easy to distinguish: he was thorough in all things and the brown tweeds camouflaged him almost too well. Howard high-stepped through an intervening clump of seedlings, but Alex stayed where he was, perched on a shooting stick in the sepia light. Only when a few yards separated them did he stand, raising his hat, producing his smile.

"Good afternoon, Howard."

Howard nodded, hand extended. "Hallo, Alex."

Without another word Howard extracted his report from the shaft of the 4-iron. Alex took it from him and shoved it immediately into an inside pocket "Good?" he asked.

"As good as I could get."

Their voices were low, dying instantly on the air. There was no resonance, not even when the thunder growled.

"You chose a fine place," Alex said.

"You think so?"

"Difficult." The small eyes twinkled. "Difficult for me. A long walk."

"I'm sorry."

"And then your ball nearly killed me—rat-tat-tat from tree to tree. Are you always such a good shot?"

"I'm sorry. It was—"

"No worry, no worry." He spread his white, plump hands. "We are together—that is the important thing. How long can you stay?"

"There's no urgency."

"Here?"

"We're safe here."

Alex settled himself on the shooting stick again. "Well,

103

my friend," he said with what seemed like warmth, "how has it been with you?"

"Reasonable."

"And how was Lisbon?"

Howard was expecting him to ask; it was only natural. He explained, and Alex clucked his tongue in sympathy for Richard. There was kindness in him. Few people in his position would have been interested in preliminaries of any kind: most were as businesslike as whores, measuring their time in minutes. But Alex was different and always had been. The podgy face wasn't totally expressionless, or the voice. When he inquired into matters that were outside the limits of their relationship he seemed to do so with genuine interest.

"My friend"—he said it more often these days.

It grew darker, but the rain held off and the thunder only threatened. Howard kept an eye on the sixth tee, but nobody appeared. A quarter of an hour must have passed before Alex began to speak of where Howard should concentrate his attentions during the weeks to come.

"There is the ASLD-equipped *Daedalus*," he began. "Now in the Indian Ocean. It would be useful if we could know something about her commander—not what will be on the files, you understand. That is one thing. Another is in a quite different direction—the Rocket Propulsion Station at Aylesbury. . . ."

They separated with a handshake. It was coming up to four by then and the storm was imminent. Howard emerged from the pines with Alex's parting words fresh in his ears—"Everything you have done has been exceptional." He picked up his second ball; it would be stupid to play on. Without once glancing back he started for the clubhouse, aiming to shortcut across the fourteenth. The clouds were ugly now, black and bruised-looking. He lengthened his stride, dragging the trolley as fast as he could. Seven or eight minutes would see him under cover. Alex would cop it, though; the railway station was a good two miles and the rain was beginning in earnest, steady and vertical.

He was crossing the fourteenth fairway when the lightning struck. There was a vicious sizzling flash and the ground seemed to jump violently beneath his feet. Instinctively he threw himself flat. He wasn't expecting the thunder and he pressed against the grass as it double-pounded in his ears. Shaken, he clambered to his feet and looked about him—for what he didn't quite know. The sense of isolation was overwhelming. He grabbed the trolley's handle and broke into a stumbling run. The rain was suddenly falling in torrents. Twice more before he reached the clubhouse the lightning zipped and he flinched. Soaked and panting, teeth bared from a stitch, he finally reached the clubhouse precincts and took refuge in Brogan's shop.

The little Irishman wasn't one to suffer fools gladly. "You can't say I didn't warn you, sir." He screwed his face in disgust at an overflowing drain. "Waited until it was right on top of us, didn't it?"

Howard kept a spare shirt and trousers in his locker. He changed, delayed until the worst of the storm had passed, then drove to Hampstead, driving fast and arriving weary. He ran a lukewarm bath, poured himself a large whiskey and squatted in front of the television to catch the early news. Biafra, the Middle East, a London bank raid, a call for strike action at a motor-components factory. . . . He listened without really listening, another part of his mind reluctantly trying to decide when to call Wyndhams and what he should say.

This afternoon, near Marsden, in Surrey, a man was struck by lightning on the perimeter of Burdean Golf Course. . . .

Howard tensed.

Papers in his possession identified him as Alexandrov Donskoy, a second secretary at the Soviet embassy in London. Inquiries are proceeding. . . .

Howard's body was rigid, his stare fixed. The newsreader mouthed at him, but he didn't hear. A high-pitched ringing sound filled his skull like an alarm. For a long elastic stretch of time he was quite unable to move. Then he suddenly jackknifed, covered his mouth and blundered into the bathroom.

BOOK THREE

CHAPTER ONE

1

A kind of mercy prevented Richard from remembering too much of the first couple of weeks after the amputation. The drugged moment of discovery, the growing realization of his physical limitations, the shooting pains where no pains could possibly be, the trembling and the giddiness, the juddering flight to Lisbon—vivid cameos remained and faces stood out from the blur, Goddard's among them, Goddard who said: "We'll soon have the *Helping Hand* patched up. Don't blame yourself, whatever you do. . . ."

Lisbon was noise and weakness and uncertainty, with strained silences between himself and Howard and brief verbal forays into one another's territory. He wasn't ready for any of it. In mind and body he had longed to be done with traveling and to reach home; there was heartbreak in him. But Wyndhams was never a place of healing and his real wounds were within. The obscene horrors of Abaguma and the surrounding bush haunted his waking hours. When Tibbie wept her lukewarm tears and Howard let loose his spite he pitied them; they lacked nothing except love.

Compassion was the world's great need: the new-born howled for it and the dying cupped their hands. He hadn't always understood. There was a time when he'd abandoned the clockwork Catholicism that wound him up and put him through the motions: he'd turned to life and lived it on its own terms. But unlike Howard he didn't entirely disown the faith he had quarreled with—Rosalind had spared him that. For a while Rosalind was everything, Rosalind and the flying; he was on Canberras then. But that November, while the headlines were screaming Suez, he was born again above Kasfareet airfield, born by way of shame and self-disgust as he strafed and hunted the terrified ground crews through the smoking aftermath of his own bombing. Within minutes he was changed, changed utterly: the future he had thought of could never be the future he would know. He flew the Canberra back to Cyprus like a man who'd seen his own ghost. In the new year he left the service and the following summer he began to study for the priesthood. "You're being too hasty," his father argued sadly. "That's always your trouble—you're a spur-of-the-moment man." Tibbie had raged. "Why? Why?" And then, when his answers defeated her: "You should have gone into the Army. None of this would have happened if you'd done as I wanted."

Only Rosalind forgave him, and then with difficulty, needing her own anguish to glimpse the extent of his vision. "Good-bye." She held and kissed him for the last time. "Good-bye," she said, and watched him go.

And so he'd become what he was—"I smell incense," Howard used to mock. Time had molded him, and chance had singled him out. Thin and ravaged and tired beyond words, he arrived at Wyndhams and rested as best he could. The cottage hospital removed his stitches. O'Sullivan poured him a sherry and told him that, God willing, Tibbie had "years yet." Howard didn't telephone. Sister Marie and Sister Assumpta and Albert Okawe ached like a cancer on his conscience. Avidly he read and listened for a mention of Abaguma, but in vain. John Wyatt, the parish priest, got wind of his presence and came to sympathize, walking with him in the garden, speaking endlessly of the pill and abortion, and celibacy and the liturgical revolution.

"You're Farrer's diocese, aren't you? Westonlake?"

"I was, so I suppose I still am."

"Have you heard from him yet?"

"No, but I've written his secretary."

A letter with a Westonlake postmark duly arrived, requesting Richard's attendance at Bishop's House on the Saturday; the wording was as opaque and impersonal as any civil servant's. Later that day a girl with nasal vowels from BBC television rang to ask whether Richard was willing to appear on *Here and Now* to answer questions on his recent experiences in Biafra—"they sound pretty fantastic to us."

"I'll answer questions on conditions there, but not about myself."

"Not on the flying bit?"

"Especially not the flying bit."

"But that's what's so great. It's really different. . . ." She fluffed his name. "There's been such a load of the other stuff recently that it's become something of a drag. Our feeling is—"

He hung up. It wasn't the only approach: the press were also onto him. Over a period of several days they pestered by telephone and by letter and in person. "No," he told them. "No, I'm sorry—I've nothing to say." It didn't stop them sneaking a photograph of him when he happened to leave the house and putting a few professionally emotive pieces together, but they dropped him soon enough.

"Good riddance," Tibbie said when the calls no longer came. "What business was it of theirs?"

Westonlake meant a train journey, with a change at Guildford. Bishop's House stood at one end of a Georgian terrace which faced onto a public green. The hall floor was covered with red linoleum and a picture of the Sacred Heart greeted the visitor. Nothing much had changed; the enclosed space still reeked of polish and the slanting bars of sunlight were empty of dust.

The housekeeper showed him to the waiting room. He had hardly sat himself down when Monsignor Brace, the bishop's secretary, entered through another door. He was a stranger to Richard, nervous and gray-haired, equipped with a crushing handshake.

"The bishop will see you now, father."

He ushered Richard into the book-lined room and Bishop Farrer rose behind his crowded desk to greet him.

He was a small, nondescript man with a reputed passion for tennis.

"Glad to see you again, Father Lawrence—though I'm distressed at what has happened—most distressed."

"My lord."

"It's taken a lot out of you, I can see." He indicated the chair on Richard's side of the desk. "Please."

"Thank you."

The bishop's gaze flickered over a note placed on his blotting pad. "How long ago did this dreadful thing take place?"

"Almost three weeks, my lord."

"And you've been home—"

"A week. A week today."

"Ah." Another downward glance. The voice was dry and crumbling. "At Marsden?"

"That's correct."

"How do you manage . . . with the one arm?"

"I'm restricted, naturally. Just how—and when—I'm learning as I go along."

"Of course." The bishop cleared his throat. A number of press clippings were also on the desk and he riffled through them. "You've attracted quite an amount of publicity, I see."

"Not intentionally."

"These days it's almost inevitable, I'm afraid, and yours could have been a deal more sensational; so we must be thankful for small mercies." He smiled weakly, skin deep. "Nevertheless, despite what I've read, I must confess to being slightly in the dark, father. I wonder if you would be so good as to answer a few questions?"

Richard hadn't expected an easy interview. "Certainly, my lord."

"Did you obtain permission to leave your parish in Biafra?"

"No."

"Why was that?"

"It wasn't possible. All communication had broken down. We were absolutely cut off."

"Why, then, did you leave?"

"In an attempt to get help, my lord."

109

Lips pursed, the bishop gazed at his locked fingers.

"My original intention," Richard said, "was to return within forty-eight hours. I went to a neighboring town where there was an airstrip, but the relief people there had more than enough on their hands as it was." A thousand times faster than speech he thought of the lean American and the moaning outside the stifling hut and Sharkey and the rain and the mission's Land Rover left on the broken road with a label tied to it like a flag of defeat. "The only chance, it seemed to me, was to get to São Tomé and explain the seriousness of Abaguma's situation to the various relief organizations' headquarters."

"Abaguma?"

"Abaguma was my parish."

"Was?" The bishop tilted his narrow head. "Was, father? The truth of the matter, surely, is that you have abandoned it."

"Abandoned is a monstrous word to use, my lord."

"I am referring to what is an obvious fact; not to your well-meaning—though misguided—motives."

"Misguided?"

"Your duty was to those you had chosen to serve."

"My lord, the people I had chosen to serve were—and still are—dying for lack of food and medical supplies." Richard's voice had a cutting edge. "They are dying in conditions of such unutterable squalor that you would be appalled. In the hospital compound, where two sisters of the Society of the Incarnation and a local doctor struggle to do what they can, the stench is such that you would hate to draw breath. My duty was to insure that something positive was done to save the town and district from total disaster."

"With no thought of the consequences?"

Somewhere in the house a clock chimed. Richard paused, listening to its soft indifference. "I can assure you, my lord, that I would rather be in Abaguma than here. But I can also assure you that for me to be physically present in Abaguma would do nothing to help the living. The dying, yes; but my concern is also for the living." He stared unblinking at the man—the good man—on the other side of the desk in the neat, dustless room, knowing

110

that he could never pierce his prudent and theological approach to the terrible human calamity that was Biafra. "Because of the living I went to São Tomé, but help was hard to come by. There are many Abagumas, my lord. Because of the living I flew that plane, and if we hadn't been hit I would have gone on flying it until its pilot was well enough to take over. Then, and only then, I would have returned to Abaguma. To return was always my intention."

"And now?"

"Now, my lord?"

"Now," the bishop nodded. "What are your intentions now?"

"I'm in no position to answer. Strictly speaking I have eight months of my offered three years abroad still to complete."

"Quite."

The silence between them was deep and lasting. Eventually the bishop pushed back his chair. He stood up and went to the window, where something in the street seemed to hold his interest.

"Have you managed to say mass since you arrived home?"

"With difficulty."

"Where?"

"At Marsden. With the parish priest's permission."

"A public mass?"

Richard shook his head. "No."

"An approach has to be made to Rome on your behalf," the bishop said. "Because of your disability. Were you aware of that?"

"I wasn't sure."

"I ask because you are obviously precluded from certain activities by reason of your handicap. However, parish work ought to be within your capability, and I have no fear of Rome raising any objection." The bishop returned to his desk. "Do you know Evensham, father?"

"Only by name."

"South of here—Father Somerset, Daniel Somerset. He's badly in need of a curate. You could go there on a temporary basis."

"When, my lord?"

"Next week?"

"Very well."

"Father Somerset will be delighted. For the present, though, you should say your masses privately and limit what you undertake in other directions." The bishop rounded the desk and held out his hand. "Good-bye, father. You have my sympathy and my blessing. I am perfectly sure your motives were impeccable, but to mean well is no excuse. We must discipline ourselves—always and everywhere. What would happen if we all did as we individually thought best? Peter, you remember, only managed to cut off an ear."

Coldly, Richard kissed the ring.

"These are difficult days, trying times, for all of us in the church. Evensham, like everywhere else, will have its own special problems. Try not to rush at them like a bull at a gate. Think, father. Advice is always to be had. Think and ask."

He came with Richard to the front door, a door which seemed to have shut out the world: he was said to be a fine administrator.

"Good-bye, my lord."

Richard's heart was like stone. The first rules of the church were those she hadn't made herself. Life was more than a desiccated intellectual exercise. Life was precious and love was yourself in others and others in yourself: he knew it in his bones, in his flesh. There were no asterisks, no temporizing footnotes. The world cried out for a true humanity under the transcendence of God— for rest and peace and pardon. He walked in the sunshine to the station, walking slowly, more disturbed than at any time since he became a priest.

On the morning he left Wyndhams for Evensham his mail included a letter from Exeter.

Dear Father Lawrence, he read. *I am writing on behalf of the sponsors and organizers of the* Helping Hand *venture to thank you for so gallantly putting our DC 3 to use in Biafra earlier this month. We have had a full*

112

report from **Mr. Goddard** *of your dangerous flight and a detailed summary of the damage to the plane from Mr. Dunlop, who is happily recovered from his illness.*

We are sure you will be pleased to learn that repairs have now been effected and that the DC 3 is once again airworthy. Permission for additional relief sorties has unfortunately not yet been granted, but Mr. Dunlop and Mr. Goddard are more anxious for you to know that they are pressing the claims of Abaguma and district in their applications.

In the meantime all connected with Helping Hand *sincerely trust that you are making a steady return to health after the tragic. . . .*

It had the touch of a parish magazine, but he forgave the stilted phrasing. He was grateful. They might very well have taken a different line. He'd made use of them and unofficial bodies weren't normally so forgiving. But in other ways the letter tore at his heart. International bureaucracy would one day choke the world to death.

"Good-bye, mother. I'll be back to see you as soon as I can." The market had fallen and Tibbie was surly, put out. "Remember—you're only to telephone if you want me."

Evensham was neat and tidy, red brick and gray stone, ringed by light industry. "Glad to see you, father," Daniel Somerset greeted him. "Glad to have you here. Thank God you got to Bishop Farrer when you did. If it had been the Wimbledon fortnight we'd have both been waiting yet." He was a big, bald, jovial individual with bushy brown eyebrows. "Come in, come in, and let's hear all about you."

In the cramped study he drew Richard's story out of him, listening intently, nodding, often nodding—"And then?" he would ask. "And then? . . ." His quick eyes never lacked interest. Several times he whistled. "Fantastic," he kept saying. "Fantastic." And when it was done he leaned back and lit his pipe. "Well, I'll tell you this, father. You'll meet with a lot of personal sympathy but precious little real understanding. For the majority Biafra is a headline taken between mouthfuls, as it were.

113

There's no shock wave. It's too far away. For a small proportion it's worth demonstrating about. But as for doing something positive, actually *doing* something—well now, that really makes you quite a curiosity, father." The smoke swirled. "Apathy isn't for Biafra alone, you understand. It's currently for everywhere except the moon and for everything except the football results. On top of it all the young have got the bit between their teeth but don't know where they're going. I won't bore you, but that's the way the country is right now and Evensham's a part of it. Something's gone at the roots." He clucked his tongue, then brightened. "Another word and you'll turn about and run. Wouldn't blame you, either—this is no way to get started. . . . Do you drink Guinness?"

Two days later he came to Richard's room. "Have you seen the *Times*?"

His expression was a warning of what to expect. With trepidation and dismay Richard almost snatched the paper from him. Endlessly he had looked and listened for a mention of Abaguma and now it was there: *Within the shrinking boundaries of the Ibo heartland a fresh atrocity has been inflicted on a stricken people from the air. . . .* His eyes read over the lines. An Ilyushin, high-explosive and antipersonnel bombs. Direct hits on mission hospital. International Red Cross observers helicoptered in. Scenes of utmost horror. *Two nuns of the Society of the Incarnation and the Mission's doctor are among the fifty-three known dead. . . .*

The print blurred. He looked up and stared through Daniel Somerset, struck dumb, grief blinding him, filling him, fists of rage beating in anguish against his tangled senses. His lips moved but nothing came. He rocked a little, eyes closed, remembering everything, everything, imagining the feeble desperation of camp and compound nudged by a distant droning into a renewal of hope.

"They would have thought it was another food drop." He made small distracted motions with his right hand. "They would have thought it was going to be like the other time. Wouldn't they? I mean—wouldn't they?"

His voice broke. He turned away and wept for them, racked by the spasms.

114

CHAPTER TWO

1

In the near-panic of Thursday evening Howard had rid himself—with one exception—of everything that might damn him. The typewriter he buried in a field behind a lay-by near Watford, the cipher pad he burned, the cigarette case he tossed into the Thames from the Embankment. He drove miles that night, back and forth. He almost burned his false passport as well, but he kept his head and left it hidden in the invisible recess in his bookshelves: it could be his lifeline.

He didn't doubt they'd come to him. There were others at DNI who handled the kind of classified information that came his way, others who could have typed the report Alex had on him, but there was no one else with a family home within a mile of Burdean. And Brogan had seen him, talked with him—before and after. Brogan would confirm the times. They'd come, all right.

He was at his desk next morning as usual, the ulcerous ache of his nerves masked over, half watching his door, half afraid of the phone, wondering, all the time wondering. Starey sauntered in early on. "Rum affair this Russian chap yesterday, don't you think? Down your way, wasn't it? Lightning of all things—now there's a turn up." He tapped his pockets as if feeling himself for damp, and when Howard offered him a cigarette from a pack he said: "What's happened to your case? Lost it?" It was a nightmare of a day. In late afternoon Starey spoke to him again. "There's word going around," he said with worried disbelief, "that the Russian killed at

Burdean had ASLD information on him—actually on him. May not be true, of course. But if it is then it's bad, bad for all of us."

Howard didn't leave the flat that evening. He ate little and drank nothing, believing he would need a clear head and a sure tongue. But nobody came. Nobody came that night or on the Saturday. Why? Without ceasing he questioned himself. Everything pointed in one direction—a child could have seen it. Yet Saturday passed and kept him in suspense, ready for them, willing them to come. They could prove nothing. Suspect, yes; prove, no. He argued his case, over and over. Deliberately he followed an ordinary Saturday pattern—shopping locally in the morning, the Black Rabbit around noon, cleaning the car after lunch—and the sense of isolation grew. It was unnerving to be so alone, so ignored, and not to have Alex a message away any more, Alexandrov Donskoy who had promised him safety. "Don't worry, don't worry. You will be looked after. . . ."

By whom? Contact was broken. In that direction, too, he was at the mercy of others to make a move.

June was away for the weekend, otherwise she might have distracted him. He called Wyndhams during the afternoon, somehow hoping that Richard's calm might be contagious, but found himself forced to endure Tibbie instead. The threat of a cat-and-mouse Sunday drove him in desperation to thumb through his notebook in search of the Redhill number: like it or not he had to be where he once belonged. Jessica answered.

"It's me," he said.

Her surprise was icy. "Why, hallo."

"Are you at home tomorrow?"

"I don't know. I haven't thought yet. I don't usually—"

"I'd like to come down."

"All of a sudden?"

"I'm sorry if it seems like that."

"I'll have to ask the children. I'm never sure what their plans are."

Pride was a thing of the past. "Just let me come. Around midday. We could lunch somewhere."

"Will you wear something to identify yourself? You

116

know—so that the children don't make fools of themselves?"

Bitch, he thought. For a moment his mind swirled. Then anxiety possessed him again—knowing that he was compromised and knowing that they knew, *must* know, yet still did nothing. Surely they knew? . . . But for Burdean he could have begun to doubt it: several Ministry of Defense establishments were aware of ASLD; it wasn't a DNI monopoly. Burdean, however, upset the odds.

He drove to Redhill through the Sunday southbound traffic. The sense of unreality was very strong and his mind couldn't settle. Jessica was hardly a refuge, yet he was using her as one and he couldn't quite reason why; he should have made for neutral ground. He took two wrong turns before finding the house. He'd lost his way on other occasions, but he didn't this time admit to it. Accidentally his elbow sounded the horn as he was getting out of the car. Barefoot, in a green front-buttoned cotton dress, Jessica came around the side of the house.

"We're at the back," she said, offhand but waiting for him. "It's so hot."

"You look well." He heard himself. "You're as brown as a berry."

"That's more than I can say for you."

"I don't have your advantages."

"You really ought to choose your words more carefully."

She had her sword already drawn. He swallowed, unwilling to row. He hadn't come to row. God alone knew what he'd come for, but it wasn't for that. "Can't we at least start the way we intend to go on?"

"I thought we had," she said.

He followed her along the narrow strip of grass. "Ann," she called. "Clare. . . . You father's here."

They were by the big chestnut, playing badminton. Clare dropped her racket and came running; Ann followed more slowly. "Daddy, daddy"—Clare approached with outstretched arms and he lifted her, swinging her around. Ann he kissed, bending; her lips touched his cheek but no more.

"My, you're growing up," he said.

She was tall for her age, fair and wide-eyed and full-lipped like her mother. The eyes were accusing. Clare was a smaller, darker version of her sister, less withdrawn.

"My cat's dead," she announced.

"Dead? How sad. When did—?"

"Last month. He was run over. Mummy says he's gone to Jesus. Do you think he's gone to Jesus?"

"Your mother wouldn't tell you a lie, would she?"

"But what," Clare asked, "does Jesus want with a dead cat?"

She ran away, laughing. "Go and play with her, Ann," Jessica said. "Finish your game."

"We'd finished."

"Well, play another."

Reluctantly Ann left them. It was a neat, immaculate house with a small untidy garden, mainly lawn. A light slatted table and some folding chairs were placed on the paved area outside the French windows.

Jessica said: "What will you drink?"

"Something long. Gin and tonic will do."

She went inside. He watched the girls patting the shuttlecock over and into the net and wondered if Special Branch were in his flat. They may have wanted him out of the way; it was possible. But they wouldn't find the passport, not in a week's searching, and nothing else could bring him harm—not there.

Jessica came back with a tray. "Ice and lemon?"

"You know," Howard said.

"Tastes change." She sat facing him across the table and looked him over clinically. "Cheers."

"Good luck."

"Why are we so honored?"

Howard shrugged. "I thought it was high time."

"For my sake or the girls'?" She sipped at her glass. "Or yours?"

"I don't think I'm that analytical."

"It's a pity."

"Oh?"

"You might have unraveled yourself by now." She

paused, blue eyes in the sun-brown face. "For your own good and the good of others."

"Cut it out, will you?"

He offered her a cigarette and the absence of the case tugged at his mind; even amidst the sounds of summer and the laughter of his own children there was no escape. The lighter's flame was almost invisible in the sunlight. Through the slow smoke on the still air he gazed at Jessica and thought of their time together, about Ann and Clare, but it all seemed to have happened to someone else. She was still beautiful, but he wasn't curious about other men, or even the absence of them.

"The kids look well," he remarked.

"They're fine. They sometimes talk about you." She waved an insect away. "It's only fair to say 'sometimes'— fair to you, I mean. You don't exactly fill their lives any more."

"Did I ever?"

"That's for you to answer."

He shrugged.

"You would have felt something, you see." Her glance was withering. "That's what it's all about."

He drank, nervous and insecure and barely hiding it. "Where shall we lunch?"

"Here," she said. "It's easier here—d'you mind? Then I needn't change. A salad will be no trouble—provided you aren't in a tearing hurry."

Howard gestured indifferently. "Whatever you say."

"Tell me about Richard." Jessica drew on her cigarette. "He's had a rough time, I gather."

"Pretty bad. He might have been all right if he hadn't forgotten he was a priest."

"I'd say that was the very thing he remembered."

"He hasn't talked about it much, but he all but asked for what he got. I went out to Lisbon to bring him home."

"Where's home?"

"In his case, Marsden."

"And in yours?"

He didn't reply. He got up and walked to where the girls were playing. "Can I join you? Who's winning? . . . How about the two of you taking sides against your

119

father?" Clare was instantly in favor but Ann was cool. "Come on," he tried. "Your mother tells me you can play a real blinder." Desperately he wanted to involve himself with them. Jessica was useless; every glance as good as cut him dead. "Is there another racket? Who'll serve first—you? Your side?"

He hustled them like an auctioneer. They started the game. The small garden was full of his enthusiasm and Clare's laughing. Jessica watched them critically for a while before going into the house. "Good shot, Ann! What's the score?" He raced about, but whatever he sought eluded him and what he most feared remained. Alexandrov Donskoy: without him he was marooned. Somehow he must pick his way through the questioning, brazen out the suspicions.

Ann smashed beyond his reach. "Game!" She tossed her racket triumphantly aside. Clare ran to the house, shouting: "We beat daddy, we beat daddy." Howard followed, mopping his face. He found Jessica in the kitchen and her expression mocked him.

"Haven't you left it a bit late in the day?" she said, and if there was any remnant of satisfaction remaining to him it was that she knew so little when she believed she knew so much.

He left in the quiet of early evening. Jessica remained on the offensive to the very end and he realized what a vain hope it was to have expected better. Only Clare kissed him when he said good-bye. "Don't you mean *au revoir?*"

"I'm off my head," he said. "Of course I mean *au revoir.*"

He made good time to the flat. Were they there? Had they been? The nearer he came the more he asked himself. He wouldn't have been surprised if someone had been waiting for him in the entrance lobby or on the third floor landing or even in the flat itself. But no. And no one had been inside—the cotton was intact.

Relief was short-lived. Suspicion, confusion—either was more realistic, and they took hold of him afresh. Three days without even a tail, nothing in the papers since the first brief references on the Friday morning. *Inquiries are proceeding.* . . . Where, for God's sake? In which direction? "This Russian chap. . . . Down your way, wasn't it?"—when Starey had spoken to him he should have told him he was on the course at the time. There weren't many cards for him to play and he'd fluffed that one; he saw it now and could have kicked himself. Better, far better, that he should have been open about his whereabouts, informed the police, showed willing. It could only have been to his advantage. As it was he would need to explain his silence about Burdean on top of everything else.

He took his unease to bed with him and woke to find it waiting. He traveled to Whitehall with a kind of dread, but the office seemed normal enough; Starey was in his treadmill groove, inclined to play down his Friday afternoon disclosure, and Miss Chancellor's skirt was up to her bottom. It wasn't until about eleven that Howard spotted the absence of two Portland signals from the ASLD file. The index numbers had CANCELED written against them, but he wasn't fooled: canceled signals were normally kept on record. He'd expected a tap on the shoulder, a knock on the door; to be confronted would have been preferable. But a nod was as good as a wink. They were onto him. There was no mistake; the signals were missing by design, by order. It was a defensive reaction that told its own tale and for years he'd watched for it.

His fingers trembled as he lit a cigarette. Starey would be aware of the order, yet he hadn't so much as blinked an eye. Others would be aware of it too, others in the same building. Suddenly he was among enemies.

The man who had brought it all on him was the man he now needed most: but Alex was dead and all he could do was sweat it out alone.

He hadn't much longer to wait. He'd hardly reached home when someone came to the door, a square-shouldered man with pinched cheeks and wet blue eyes. He was so close on Howard's heels that he must have been on the lookout for him.

"Commander Lawrence?"

"That's right."

"Andrew Garner." He showed his warrant card as if it were a season ticket. "May I come in?"

"Of course." Howard led him through to the living room, outwardly calm, his reactions drilled. "Is this by any chance to do with Burdean and that Russian embassy official?"

"You sound as if you've been expecting me."

"Yes and no. Can I get you anything—scotch?"

"No, thank you."

"Cigarette?"

"I've given them up, thanks." He sounded slightly smug.

Howard indicated a chair. "Please," he said, and Garner took his time, eyes on the go, lifting his trouser creases over his thick knees.

"Could you explain what you meant by yes and no?"

"Simply that I wasn't sure whether you would come or not—'you' being Special Branch."

"Why did you suppose we might?"

"Isn't that obvious?"

"To you, perhaps." An awful little smile with a total lack of meaning. "Perhaps you would enlighten me."

Howard paused. "Just how official is your visit?" He spoke lightly but with extreme care. "I think I've a right to know what legal authority you have to question me. Not that I much mind, but for curiosity's sake—"

"The same authority which gives me the right to examine your bank statements, search this flat and your possessions and relieve you of your passport."

Howard laughed. "You've got all *that?*"

"If need be, commander."

"My God."

The smile flickered again. "It's a right not often exercised. Now, you were saying—?"

"I was saying I half expected to be interviewed in view of the fact that I was playing golf at Burdean around the time the Russian was killed."

Garner fingered the side of his nose. "You think a coincidence of that order sufficient to bring me here?"

"If your people are doing a job of work, yes. Particularly in view of what the Russian had on him."

"Which was?"

"ASLD data?" The inflection was deliberate. "Captain Starey told me as much."

"What else did he tell you?"

"Nothing relevant that I remember."

"When did you hear of Donskoy's death?"

"The Russian? That evening, on BBC television news."

"And you did nothing?"

"I don't understand."

"Did you mention your having been on the course at the material time to anybody?"

"No."

"You thought it unnecessary?"

"I did."

"Even thoough you are currently serving in the Directorate of Naval Intelligence?"

"Yes."

"And have access to classified ASLD information?"

"Yes."

"And consider yourself a submarine specialist?"

"That's as may be. I repeat, I knew nothing about the Russian having ASLD information until Captain Starey informed me."

"When was that?"

"Friday afternoon."

"And you still took no action? It never entered your head to contact the authorities?"

"If someone were murdered in this block I very much doubt if I would go the police simply because I live here."

"That's hardly a fair analogy, commander."

"Perhaps not," Howard conceded. "What I'm saying is that I've by no means exclusive knowledge of ASLD. There must be a couple of hundred people as close to it as myself and a fair number a good deal closer."

"Not one of whom was at Burdean that day. Not one, that is, except you."

Howard shrugged. "It's my home course. I'm there often enough."

"Playing alone?"

"Sometimes. You can easily check."

Garner shifted position. "Am I correct in believing that at no time since Thursday evening have you considered the onus was on you to disclose your whereabouts that day? Would that be a fair summary of your attitude?"

"My whereabouts were already known."

"To whom?"

"Brogan."

"You consider this is how a responsible officer should behave?"

"I'm merely answering questions about myself in given circumstances."

Garner frowned. "You don't consider yourself responsible?"

"I'm sorry," Howard said with a trace of bite, "but I'm not used to these verbal parlor games. Of course I consider myself responsible. And I emphatically deny that I'm in any way the cause of ASLD information being in a dead Russian's possession."

"Despite your proximity to him at the material time?"

"You yourself mentioned coincidence."

"So I did," Garner acknowledged. "Did I also mention exactly what ASLD data Donskoy was found to be carrying?"

"No."

"Does it surprise you to know that it was taken verbatim from a Portland signal on the most recent ASLD trial?"

"It does indeed."

"When Captain Starey broke the news to you on Friday afternoon weren't you anxious to find out what caliber of information had gone astray?"

"Naturally."

"Did you ask him?"

"He'd got wind of a rumor—no more than that. He wasn't in a position to give details."

"It worried you, though?"

"Of course."

"Over the weekend?"

"Among other things."

"Did you raise the matter with him today?"

Howard nodded. "As far as he was concerned it was still hearsay. He tended to discount it."

"And you still saw no reason to mention where you were on Thursday?"

"No."

"What else worried you over the weekend?"

"Family affairs."

Garner rubbed his knees with the flat of his hands. "Donskoy had a typewritten report which also included matters unrelated to ASLD."

"Such as?"

"Policy decisions, strategic pros and cons. . . . The information has all been on the your desk in recent days."

"Not only mine."

"Granted, commander. But I am sure you must see that, taken all in all, it was inevitable you would be subjected to questioning."

"I've nothing to hide. You can ask all you want."

Garner was almost apologetic. "It may take some time."

"I don't mind—so long as we can eat." Howard thought he played it just right. "There's a small place up the hill I usually go to. Perhaps you'll join me?"

"Later, if you don't mind. Before we do that, however—before we go any further, in fact—I must ask you to let me have your passport."

It came out of the blue, without change of tone or facial expression and for a second or two Howard was caught off guard.

Recovering, he said. "You must be joking."

"Voluntary action on your part will spare you what I'm sure would be unwelcome publicity." The vapid smile hovered momentarily. "Relieving you of your passport is nothing more than an elementary precaution."

"A bloody insulting one."

"Inevitably. But it stands to reason."

"Am I suspended from duty?"

"That's not within my power to say."

"Asking for my passport is?"

Garner nodded. "The alternative's a legally enforced demand. Call your solicitor if you don't believe me."

Howard gave him a long stare of simulated protest. "This is absolutely preposterous."

"I'm sure I would feel the same in your shoes."

"When will I get it back?"

"When our inquiries are complete."

"How long will that be?"

"I can't really say."

"Jesus Christ!" Howard stormed into the other room, returning a couple of minutes later with his genuine passport. He flipped it at Garner, making him reach. "Now what?"

Garner gazed up at him. "Now, immediately now, I want to go back to last Thursday."

"And then?"

"Then, commander, I should like to ask a few questions about your career in general—about Korea, for instance, about Naples, about Lisbon. . . ."

Garner left at midnight, polite to the last. They didn't eat, either there or up the hill. More than once he laid traps which Howard avoided. He was never subtle but worked repeatedly over the same ground, trying the patience, relying it seemed on an exasperated slip of the tongue or a variation of answer. Howard was exhausted by the time he showed him out, but he experienced something close to a sustainable relief before he slept.

They could suspect all they liked but nothing could be proved. Only a fluke, a million to one chance, had put them onto him, and nothing like it would happen again. They could zigzag at will through his career, but he had always been meticulous; there were no loose ends. From now on nothing could ever be the same as before, but in time they would surely be forced to admit defeat, call off the tail, return what was his. Until that happened he must risk nothing, contact nobody, cling to all the confidence he could generate within himself.

Others had walked a razor's edge and survived, and so could he.

BOOK FOUR

CHAPTER ONE

1

He was not suspended. Nobody summoned him and told him to stay clear of the office. But there was noticeably less on his desk, and in midmorning Miss Chancellor brought him a message to the effect that the Tuesday meeting of the Interservices Liaison Committee had been canceled—nonsense, of course. It was unnatural to rub shoulders and yet to feel isolated, not knowing which of his colleagues were aware that he was under investigation and which of them therefore lied to his face, covered up, withheld information. Starey he was sure of, but only Starey. Starey wasn't at ease with pretense; he didn't quite look at him anymore.

Garner's visit hung over the day like a cloud, and when Howard returned to Hampstead he found the strand of cotton broken and knew that the flat had been searched. But for the cotton they had made a first-class job; hardly anything was more than fractionally out of place. And they'd been thorough to the point of having the carpet up. He walked around, checking, consoled only by the thought that they could have searched for a week and still wasted their time. There *was* nothing—nothing except his other passport, and this was encased in the wood of the floor-to-ceiling bookshelves; its recess gloss-painted over, apparently nonexistent. If ever he wanted to open it up he would need a chisel.

He wasn't followed from Whitehall, but a man loitered near the drive-in to the flats when Howard arrived, and he was still there a couple of hours later. It was odd how they did some things so well and others with such ham-fisted obviousness: Howard watched him with a kind of derision. Alex's last instruction had been to make use of a dead-letter box in Regent's Park and he certainly wasn't going there; he wasn't going anywhere that could possibly give Garner any satisfaction.

June rang him, spluttering with hay fever. "How long have you had that?" he asked.

"Since the weekend. It's murder."

"I can believe it."

"Did the fellow call?"

"What fellow?"

"About typewriter accessories."

Howard tensed, alerted. "I'm not with you."

"If I hadn't been feeling so lousy I wouldn't have suggested—"

"Can you start at the beginning?" It was enormously difficult to sound casual. "I haven't got the picture at all."

"There was a fellow at the door selling typewriter ribbons and carbon papers." June sounded as if she was in tears. "We weren't any use to each other and I told him so. Then he asked if I knew anyone in the block who might be interested—to save his legs, I suppose—and I said you."

"When was this?"

"An hour ago. I didn't mean to throw him into your lap, but I'm bunged up to the eyes and just wanted to get rid of him."

"You told him I'd got a typewriter?"

" 'Fraid so." She gave a smothered laugh. "And when I ring to apologize I find he never bothered."

Howard's stare was unfocused. Yesterday Garner had said to him: "Have you by any chance a typewriter, commander?" It was late then, around eleven; the cold empty craters of the moon were on display outside the windows and he was tired beyond words. "A typewriter?" he'd countered. "No—I haven't had one in years."

Christ, he thought. What else would they question? Who else?

He gazed at the man in the street below: Garner was the thin edge of the wedge and they seemed to know so much already; where to go. "I saw you," June had once said. "Up near the pond. . . ." Suddenly he was scared again, scared in all manner of ways, with and without reason, just when he fancied he had mastered himself and could ride the crisis out.

2

"Howard?"

"Hallo, Richard." This was at the office. "I hear you've landed in Evensham."

"A fortnight ago, yes. Listen when did you last see Tibbie?"

"When we were there together."

"Not since then?"

"No. Why?"

"O'Sullivan rang me this morning. It's her heart."

"An attack?"

"No, but she's pretty low. I was with her a day or two back and I thought she'd slipped quite a bit. When d'you think you can get down?"

"Tonight?"

"Okay. I'll see you there."

Howard taxied to Waterloo and took the train to Marsden. A lanky individual in a check jacket kept track of him all the way. He must have been new to it because he stayed far too close and at Marsden, where only one taxi was waiting, Howard had the perverse pleasure of asking him whether he wanted to share. He smiled grimly as the man declined. Where, for God's sake, did they imagine he was going? Did they somehow expect him to betray himself under their very eyes—and so soon?

Mrs. Wood opened the door and let him in, surprised; he'd forgotten to tell her he was coming. He stood in the must-smelling hall acclimatizing his eyes to the gloom.

"Is my brother here?"

"Not yet, Mr. Howard. He said he'd arrive about seven." Another half hour. "I think you'll find your mother has gone downhill quite a bit, Mr. Howard. Not in any dramatic way. Quietly, very quietly, over the last week. You'll notice a change in her, I'm sure."

The stairs protested under his weight. He paused, as usual, outside her room like a swimmer about to plunge, remembering how his father had tiptoed cautiously past whenever Tibbie was resting. He tapped and entered.

"Hallo, Tibbie darling." He took her hand, kissed her cheek; the bones were as fragile as a bird's. "How's my girl?"

"Tired," she said. "So tired."

"It's the heat. Everybody's feeling it."

She moved her head from side to side on the high pillows. "The heat doesn't worry me. Old age does."

"Nonsense."

Her gaze defied him. "It isn't nonsense."

She seemed to have wilted. There wasn't a blemish on her face or a line that she had earned, yet something had gone. She was limp and listless and her eyes had lost their feverbright glint. He sat on the side of the bed and flattered her, teased her, handling her in the only way he knew how, the way he'd devised to placate her will and spare himself the whiplash of her tongue. Revenge he had taken elsewhere.

"Richard's coming, did you know?"

"I forget . . . I think so. But I wasn't expecting you."

"I'm ashamed of myself, darling. I should have been here last week."

He thought of Burdean and the crackling zip of the lightning flash. One thing was sure; they'd never question Tibbie. She appeared in his personal file along with Richard and Jessica and the names of his father and his children and the details of his service and the dates he'd been security vetted. But what they were after—and where to get it—wasn't to be found there. "Examine my record," he'd said to Garner. "When this is over, when you've finished making fools of yourselves, I'm going to expect an apology—in writing," and Garner had replied, "I should imagine you would, commander."

Sunlight dappled the room. In the photograph beside

the bed his father stood very erect and looked very proud, as if the uniform demanded it of him. There had always been a uniform at Wyndhams, but the major had never heard a shot fired in anger; all his battles had been with Tibbie and most of them were ignominious defeats. How safe, how impregnable, her world had been. She had dictated its terms and had offered no quarter. With that in mind Howard could observe the silver-gray hair and china-blue hands and note the change in her without emotion.

It was a relief to hear the doorbell and to know that Richard had arrived. He went eagerly to the top of the stairs to greet him, more eagerly than he realized, like a man who sought a friend.

"She's not too bad," he said. "I'm sure it's the heat as much as anything."

"O'Sullivan doesn't think so."

He followed Richard into the bedroom and watched him kiss her, envying as before the ease of his approach and the degree of his concern. It made him feel uncomfortable. Richard possessed a kind of strength that had never come his way; it seemed to grow the more life used him. Howard ran his tongue over his lips, trying to remember what it was like to have something to fall back on instead of another version of himself. He had wheedled God in his time, but not for more than half his span of years, and then to no avail. Prayer meant belief, and he didn't believe. Early on, even as a born, trained Catholic, God had seemed to him a myth. Life was labyrinth enough without those intricate, dogmatic mysteries, without the obligation of guilt and grief and grace, without the fretting for union with something nonexistent and unknowable. Reality had its own needs and made its own demands. The vast horizonless silence of space was useless when the pressure was on; past experience told him so.

He managed to catch Richard's eye and, after a while, they went downstairs. "How are things with you?"

"Evensham isn't exactly the most exciting place on earth."

"Personally, I meant." Talking was like a drug that kept his mind from where it least wanted to go.

"Oh, I'm getting along." Richard smiled ruefully. "I don't reel about as much as I did or knock so much over."

"Any news of Abaguma?"

"It was bombed."

"When?"

"Last week."

"Badly?"

"To death." Richard's voice thickened. "Most of the papers carried the story."

"I don't remember seeing anything." How did one answer? Howard glanced hurriedly at the empty sleeve. "I'm sorry." It was easier to look Richard in the face, in the eyes—something he rarely did to anyone. But your arm, he wanted to say. Your arm, man. What about your arm? . . . He knew something about self-control, yet he marveled at Richard's. How much of what he felt was battened down? He began again: "I don't know what to say."

"Then try not to."

"Aren't you bitter?"

"I'd be a saint if I weren't. They were a part of my life."

Howard frowned; he would never read him, never understand. "Has Tibbie heard of it?"

"No." Richard shook his head. "She'd have been on at me, otherwise. I hope she never hears. To be honest, I don't think I could take her kind of 'I told you so.' "

As a distraction Howard offered him a cigarette. The squat pack was alien in his hand, reminding him of the Embankment and the plop as the waters received the gilt-rimmed case. He had lost something too. Not the case, not that. Alex. Not an arm, but Alex, an ally who had promised sanctuary if ever the need arose. He flicked his lighter under the waiting cigarette. Unmerited suffering was redemptive; the phrase lay exposed in an abandoned Catholic corner of his mind and he told himself that Richard would find solace and acceptance in its meaning. But there was no such thing as solace where the loss of Alex was concerned: only danger and loneliness.

132

There was never much subtlety in the manner they chose to withhold or divert information, and by midweek there was none at all. Whole batches of stuff weren't coming his way. He toyed for a while with the notion of asking Miss Chancellor to get him, say, the Rosyth repair schedules, curious to see what kind of excuse would be fed back to him. In the end he decided against it; nothing would be gained. It wasn't as if he didn't know about Garner: they were sidetracking him with his eyes wide open and could just as easily have decided on suspension. The moment his exclusion from certain categories of classified material showed signs of easing he reckoned he could assume the investigation was coming to an end. There was no other way of telling. Garner was hardly likely to keep him informed and their surveillance of him was no guide; it was erratic and unpredictable, sometimes in evidence, sometimes not.

Summer burned from day to day, discoloring the empty sky. The heat dulled the noise of the traffic lumbering along Whitehall and the fountains in Trafalgar Square glittered with breezeless precision. Seen through Admiralty Arch, mirages quivered in the incandescent distances of the mall and over in St. James's Park the grass was more yellow than green. Howard sometimes strolled there after lunch, crossing the lake by the bridge before retiring to the office. On the Friday he found himself showing his pass at the ground-floor checkpoint at the same time as Starey.

"Too much of a good thing, don't you think?" Starey said, blowing a bit. "My garden's like a dust bowl."

He did his best, but awkwardness showed in his eyes, a kind of withdrawal, and there was silence as the lift whirred up. Miss Chancellor had left a note on Howard's desk—*12:40. Someone rang you. Left no name, but said she'd ring again.* She? Howard cast about in his mind. It certainly wasn't Tibbie and could hardly be June—not unless Garner had been onto her again, and more directly. The thought spun around but made no sense. Beyond knowing that he was in the Ministry of Defense, June had never taxed him about his work. Jessica? Possibly, though it wasn't like her to call the office.

What kind of voice?" he asked Miss Chancellor when she eventually returned. "Young? Old?"

"Medium."

"Anything else?"

"Sexy?" she offered grudgingly.

His phone buzzed just after three o'clock. "Is that you, Howard?"

"Speaking, yes."

It wasn't the best of lines. "Are you in a guessing mood?"

He hunched his shoulders. "I'm not sure."

"Guess, anyhow."

"A clue would help."

"You weren't always so cautious. Go on—I promise not to slit your throat."

The laugh spanned the years, killing what remained of his doubts. Gillian. Gillian Shelley.

"I don't believe it," he told her, shaken. "Where are you?"

"In London."

"Whereabouts in London?"

"The Churchill."

"Since when?"

"This morning."

"You and Geoffrey?"

"Just me." She said it twice.

He pursed his lips, certain that others listened. Discretion had never been her strong suit.

"Gillian, I'm tied up at the moment. May I call you back? In an hour or so? Would that be all right?" There was a hurt silence. Pointedly he said: "How *is* Geoffrey, by the way?"

"Fine." She swept that aside. "More important, how—?"

"I really am sorry he's not with you." Howard very slightly spaced and slightly overstressed each word. "It's been such a long time."

"Howard—"

"Look," he said, teeth together, "I'll call you back—right?"

She took the hint at last. "Okay. *Che sarà sarà.*"

Miss Chancellor was correct about the quality of her voice; it hadn't changed. He frowned, uneasy at the thought of her suddenly being on his doorstep. He went to the near window and looked down, not really seeing, not really hearing, picturing her, remembering Lisbon and their first wolfish times together and the risks they had taken, the scribbled messages and the sordidness of where they had sometimes found themselves, eager and insatiable and on the brink of scandal. She was small and dark and endlessly vivacious, and when he left for Naples he knew that someone else would quickly take his place. Others had filled hers; lust never lasted.

He swore quietly. The present was tricky enough without the gratuitous reminder of a dead affair. When his nerves were in full control he was able to convince himself that he would survive the chance Alex had given them. But they were worming their way through his past and Gillian Shelley wasn't the only person he'd once upon a time made devious tracks to meet. Macerda and he had been furtive, too, and in their fashion often as hasty and crude. For safety's sake he didn't want a spotlight focused on Lisbon.

He rang her within the hour from a call box on the ground floor.

"I gather," she said with a chuckle, "I was treading on your toes a bit."

"Right."

"And that now, as they say, I can speak freely?"

"Right again."

"I've got a bone to pick."

"Oh?"

"Indeed I have."

"What sort of a bone?"

"You know very well what sort of a bone. You were in Lisbon a few weeks ago—"

"True."

"—and never even telephoned."

"I didn't even go to the embassy."

"That's no excuse."

"It was a rush visit. Private. Ask Theo Knipe."

135

"You could still have telephoned. When Geoffrey told me you'd come and gone I was furious."

"I'm sorry."

"So I should think."

"What are you doing in London?"

"Shopping, mainly."

"For how long?"

"Two or three days," she said and paused, using the silence like a baited hook.

"How are you placed tonight?" Tonight, tomorrow night—what did it matter? She would pester him otherwise; she'd done it once before. "I was wondering about dinner."

"I'd love that."

"Seven thirty?"

"Marvelous."

"The Churchill you said?"

"That's right. . . . Howard—"

"Yes?"

"It's rubbish, you know."

"What is?"

"Out of sight, out of mind."

Nothing stirred in him. There had been so many women. He took the sound of her voice up to his office, where he rested his elbows on the desk and put his knuckles to his lips, thinking, thinking. Dinner with an ertswhile colleague's wife—where was the harm in that? None. But it must stop there. He thought of June and the questions about a typewriter. There wasn't a lead they wouldn't follow, a person they wouldn't use, and Garner had enough going for him as it was.

CHAPTER TWO

1

He went home first, showered and changed, then returned to the West End by tube. It was a fifteen-minute
journey. At Warren Street he hustled from the train as
the automatic doors were sliding together and checked
that no one followed suit. "Dreaming, were you?" the
guard grinned as the train slid away. He rode to the surface on the escalator and the taxi he took to Portman
Square towed nothing special in its wake.

Encouraged, he entered the hotel and asked reception
to let Gillian know he was there. The foyer was full of
movement with people constantly coming and going and
he paced slowly from one end to the other, spared the
weight of someone's watchful scrutiny, the smoke from
his cigarette vanishing quickly in the conditioned air.

"Howard!"

He didn't recognize her—not immediately, not for a
split second. In the street he would have passed her by.

"Hallo, Gillian."

She'd aged, coarsened. Not much, but it showed—in
and around the eyes, alongside the mouth, under the
chin: one glance was enough.

"How well you look." She smiled at him eagerly, head
tilted, taking him in. "It's really fantastic."

He said the kind of thing she wanted. "You look pretty
marvelous yourself."

"It seems like yesterday, Howard."

He smiled back, hiding his feelings. Someone should

137

have told her to stop being pert; it was bearable once, but not at thirty-three. Thirty-three? There or thereabouts.

"D'you like this hotel? Comfortable?"

She nodded, eyes moving over his face.

"I thought we might eat near the river. Chelsea way."

"Whatever you say."

She was wearing a green and blue flowered ninon dress that stopped short a couple of inches above the knees, a coral necklace, with earrings and bracelet to match. Her skin was very brown and her lips were full of sensuality. In the quiet formality of the foyer it was odd to think how they had clawed at each other, struggled, lain gasping—and would again if she had her way. He steered her to the exit, their tread cushioned, his fingers touching her arm.

"Taxi, sir?"

Howard nodded, fumbling for a coin. They got in and he gave the address, then sat back.

"Cigarette?"

She shook her head. "D'you live north or south of the river?"

"North." He blew smoke. "Hampstead."

"Alone?"

"Someone comes in to clean, that's all."

She paused, the curl of her mouth calling him a liar. "Didn't you and Jessica—?"

"No," he said.

She paused again. "Funny, isn't it? I used to know so much about you."

"Who d'you know about now?"

"I don't answer questions like that."

"Why not?" he said, amused. "You ask 'em."

She laughed. "I'm curious. Women have a right to be more curious than men."

"Since when?"

"Since always."

"Fancy," he said.

Traffic lights slowed them and traffic pressed around. Howard flicked ash from his thighs. She had thickened, put on flesh—and the youth was going out of it. He

138

glanced at her from the corner of his eyes. In a year or two she would be fat, gross.

"D'you like being back in Lisbon?"

"It has its compensations."

"Where did you go to in between? Athens, was it?"

"Athens, yes."

"Enjoyable?"

"After a fashion."

She pressed against him as the taxi made a ninety-degree turn. Her perfume filled his nostrils, voluptuous and evocative, but nothing uncoiled in him; desire was dead. The Thames showed at an intersection and the driver hesitated, unsure where to turn. "Left," Howard directed. "Left and then sharp right." The Three Doves was new and off the beaten track, but crowded enough for Howard to be glad he'd booked a table. They walked through to a whitewashed terrace where clematis blotched the walls blue and a breath of air sometimes moved off the river, making the leaves tremble.

"Is this a haunt of yours?" Gillian asked. "Or are you playing safe?"

"I've been here a couple of times."

"It's nice," she said. "Cozy."

"No *fados,* I'm afraid."

"I'll survive."

Her eyes couldn't leave him alone. She drank quickly, with a kind of intent. She had three gin and tonics before dinner, by which time she was beginning to laugh too often and lean too close. In this respect, at least, she hadn't changed, but he had been blind to it before, eager himself, not caring. By the time they had eaten and he'd ordered coffee her voice was slurred. The table lamps were lit by then.

"Tell me about Geoffrey." It was a measure of his mood that he should even ask: Shelley had long since been an abstraction.

"Geoffrey?"

Howard nodded.

"What about him?"

"I hear he's now a first secretary."

"I heard something of the kind myself." She sniggered, pertness forgotten. "Do we have to?"

"It's not obligatory."

"Good." She drained the last of her wine. "I haven't seen him for a couple of days, anyhow. He's been up to his neck."

"Who with?"

"Some man."

"He wouldn't like the way you said that."

"The man's trying to sell him information."

"Interesting?"

"If it's genuine." A tug boat hooted in the shrinking distance.

"I didn't know Geoffrey wore that sort of hat."

"He does now." Loose-mouthed, Gillian gazed at him. Time was cruelest to those who could bear it least. "Perhaps I shouldn't have told you."

"In one ear and out the other."

He smiled with coolness at the animal lurking in her eyes. She had ravished him once, and not so very long ago. How many others had shadowed her face since he was last with her? A dozen? A score?

He felt her knee against his leg. "Who on earth," he said, "is trying to flog him information?"

"You were going to forget about that."

"I still am. What kind of information?"

"I'm not really meant to know."

"But you do."

"Up to a point." She moved her knee slightly. "Howard—"

"What kind of man?"

She giggled. "Are there other kinds?"

"A foreign national?"

"No."

"Who, then?" All at once he couldn't let go.

"A local, Geoffrey said."

"Portuguese?"

"Local boy makes bad," she intoned, then moistened her lips. "Well, I imagine he's a Portuguese with a name like that."

"Like what?"

140

"Macerda," she said. "Macerda or Marceda—it's one of the two.

2

Howard's skin crawled. "More coffee, sir?"—vaguely he heard but could not answer. There was noise all around the edges of his own stunned silence and fear moved in his belly like a cold breeze. Instinct had warned him what was coming. Somehow—a moment in advance of her telling him—he had known, known and yet waited to learn. Macerda. Rafael Macerda. . . . A grubby image swirled in the panic of his mind.

"What's it matter, anyhow?" Gillian was ending. "I gather a crank with an offer of something to sell isn't all that uncommon. And this one's a crank all right, the dance he's leading Geoffrey." She linked her fingers underneath her chin as if to steady herself. "May I have a cigarette?"

Howard's throat was constricted, his movements jerky. The lighter trembled in his hand. The questions every part of him strained to ask threatened to raise mirrors in which he would see himself revealed. With dread he watched the veil of smoke shift from Gillian's lamp-lit face.

"What kind of dance?"

"Oh, he's playing hard to get." Her stare was blunt. "Nothing's more tantalizing that that, as you know damned well." She was only just a trifle drunk, but obviously so. " 'Petals in the wind, petals redder than blood. . . .' " She half-sang, half-said it with a smile. "Remember that one?—remember the Miradouro?"

"Of course." He had a vision of the men's room there, Macerda waiting for him, drying his hands. "What information's he offering?"

"Who cares?"

"I do," he blurted. "It . . . it interests me."

"At this time of the evening?"

"At any time."

"Then you're out of your mind." Her glance was at

141

once scathing and enticing. "Howard—for God's sake. . . ."

"Sorry." He nodded, more in control. Later, he thought feverishly. He must worm it out of her. Garner had diminished. Disaster was suddenly about to engulf him from another quarter; even at that precise moment it could have started to landslide down.

With what he hoped she would think was zeal he said: "Just one thing more. I find it fascinating. How exactly is he playing hard to get?"

"Pay now, tell later—that kind of thing."

"Geoffrey's not falling for it, surely?"

"I haven't been present when the bargaining's gone on."

Howard settled the bill and they rose to leave. Gillian wobbled a little and snatched at his arm, clinging to it as they made their way through the inner restaurant to the street. Presently, in a taxi, she said: "This isn't the way to the Churchill." He made no reply; his mind was in a ferment but he was aware of the convulsive pressure of her hand. He went back in time to his dealings with Macerda: he should have feared him more; distrust and contempt were not enough. From the first he should have realized that Macerda would one day come out of his hole to barter what he possessed. What price was he asking? And for what, exactly what? . . .

In Tottenham Court Road Howard put an arm round Gillian's shoulder; at Camden Town his mouth opened against hers. She would know—not all, but perhaps enough. Everything was hanging by a thread. The man he had once so hungrily cuckolded had retribution within reach; a thousand or two escudos more and it was his. But Shelley was always so cautious, so mean; he didn't belong in the marketplace. How long ago had Macerda made his approach? Two days, did she say? Howard daren't ask her again, at least not yet.

Dusk had thickened into night as the taxi climbed Haverstock Hill. He paid it off at the corner of the block and walked Gillian in a shortcut across the grass, a remnant of him on the lookout for June. No one was in the entrance lobby, and when the lift opened a solitary man emerged whom he didn't recognize.

142

"Which floor?" Gillian asked. "I like driving."

"The third."

He let her into the flat and snapped on the lights, leaning against the door as she voiced her approval of the living room.

"Lovely, Howard. Fabulous. . . . Who chose it all? On second thoughts, don't tell me."

"I chose it," he said and heard himself laugh. "Don't you believe me? What will you drink?"

"I don't think I will."

"Go on. Join me."

"All right—a gin, then. Gin and tonic."

He got ice from the kitchen and she followed him there and back. Alarm kept surging over him as if he were swimming against a tide. She came to him on tiptoe and kissed him, slopping gin from her glass, brushing her lips sideways across his—"Remember?" Her eyes glittered. "Show me, then." He obliged, like a machine, Macerda in the darkness behind his closed lids. She swayed away from him and put her glass down. "You've too many doors," she said and giggled. Grimly, he propelled her toward the bedroom, unzipping her dress with practiced skill as they entered, turning her, smearing her mouth again with his. He wanted to shake the information out of her, instead of which he knew he must earn it as a reward.

"Howard. . . ."

Her breasts sagged. He pulled at his own clothes and she watched him, mistaking his urgency. The bed shook as it took their weight. She writhed beside him, her voice a groan—"Howard. . . . How long's it been, Howard?"

He reached over and switched off the light, desperate in other ways: hours had passed since she had mentioned Macerda and panic had led him in a hundred directions. Gillian's breath fanned through the darkness. He did what was expected of him and it was as if it were happening to someone else, even when her cry broke in ecstasy against the shell of his ear.

Afterward, spent and separated, their cigarettes glowing on and off, he started to ease what he needed out of her contentment, as gentle as a locksmith with her susceptibilities and potential suspicions. It took time—a remark here, a question there, nerves held hard. Again before they slept he made love to her, and again afterward—camouflaged by casual exchange and semblances of gossip—he gleaned what he could and wondered in the sticky darkness how long he'd got before it was too late.

3

Alarm filled the void that always formed in him on waking: instantly it was there, gnawing at him the moment the morning entered his eyes. Macerda had telephoned Shelley to begin with; now they were meeting. "It's all rather cloak-and-dagger," Gillian had said dreamily. "And ten to one the man's a crank. If not, then someone in the embassy has used him as a go-between to pass classified information to the Russians."

"Is that what he claims?"

"As a starter. . . . I ask you."

"I thought you said he was playing hard to get."

"So he is. Details will follow only if the price is right."

"And will it be?"

"You know Geoffrey—he trusts everybody so." There had been mockery in her yawn. "He'll need a lot of convincing before he takes it any further."

"Has he spoken to anyone about it—officially?"

"I couldn't say. I suppose he only told me because at first he thought it was a joke."

"And now?"

"He's not quite so sure." She had touched his lips with her fingertips. "Either way it's a total secret. . . . Promise?" In the end he had got it from her all at once, in the final sated minute or two before sleep dragged her under.

He ran a bath and the sound of it woke her. She wanted him again but he refused, eyeing her plump abandonment with distaste, fear prickling his mind—"Hell, it's almost nine o'clock."

"So what?"

"Be reasonable. I'm due at the office in—"

"God," she exploded. "I forgot we're in suburbia."

She sulked, slammed doors, flounced in and out; but it didn't last. By the time he'd made coffee she had recovered her poise. At a quarter to ten he rode down in the lift with her and got out the car and drove to the Churchill.

"Will you come in with me?"

"Sorry, Gillian. I'm way behind the clock already."

"Call me, then?"

"Of course. When d'you go back?"

"The day after tomorrow—early." She wrinkled her nose at him. "Don't forget. And thanks, Howard."

"Até ã vista."

He watched her vanish through the doors. She looked rather ridiculous; it was the wrong part of the day for flowered ninon. He nosed the car into the traffic and headed northward. He wasn't going to the office. First he was going to the flat, then to the West End, then to the airport, then to Lisbon. Within hours he would be there, *had* to be there. At all costs Macerda must be stopped, his tongue tied. And no one else could do it because no one else knew. If Alex had been alive it might have been different; something might have been arranged, someone called in—God knows how they fixed these things. But without him this was impossible. Without him and without the cipher pad, the dead-letter box in Regent's Park and the personal columns of the *Daily Telegraph* were useless. In any case there wasn't time. He was cut off, adrift, alone—with Garner already on his heels, Garner who had everything except the proof which Shelley might soon possess and telex home.

Howard drove toward Hampstead. He would have to kill Macerda. Appalled, a part of his mind shied from the certainty of it: inside his skin he squirmed. Overnight it had come to this. At some lights near Camden Town a van drew alongside and somebody swore at him, but he didn't hear. "Where do they meet?" he'd asked Gillian. "Where does Geoffrey go?"

He clenched his jaws and drove to the flat, his heart at freezing point. He took a chisel from the tool box in the garage and carried it up to the third floor, let himself in. The bed was still unmade and he stared at it hopelessly

145

for a moment, terrified anew by the enormity of his loneliness and the price of survival.

CHAPTER THREE

1

He cut the panel out of the bookcase and removed the passport. Bruce Elliott, company director. . . . Alex had given it to him—"Who knows?" he'd said. "Better safe than sorry. Hide it. Hide it well." Inside the passport were twenty ten-pound notes, but these were Howard's own: Macerda was the mercenary. He gazed at the man in the photograph who somehow wasn't exactly like him and fanned the pages. Mr. Elliott had traveled— Spain, France, Italy; the dates and entry points were stamped in black and violet ink. He replaced the panel in the upright and stacked some books against it, then returned to the bedroom, tidied the bed and emptied his pockets of everything that carried his name—credit cards, check book, driving license. He needed so little: cigarettes, lighter, pen, handkerchief, sunglasses, gloves. . . . It astounded him that he should foresee the need for gloves; an unknown part of him had already taken control, moving him purposefully toward nightmare.

The telephone rang, plucking his nerves. He hesitated for a while before deciding not to answer. Miss Chancellor, more than likely, checking to see if he was unwell. Strange, but over and above everything, he'd once had a career. . . . He pushed the thought away, and all those associated with it. The gloves were of light soft suede and they flattened in his trouser pocket against his right hip: he'd used them up the hill and elsewhere. Passport, cigarettes, lighter—again, like a miser, he went through what he was taking. What he was leaving he locked away. Finally he set the cotton strand across the bathroom door, then started on his journey.

He walked to the tube. Hatless, no coat, without luggage—he didn't look as though he was going far. Nobody set off in discreet pursuit, but he twice changed trains before coming up for air at Leicester Square. He took his turn in the BEA office in Lower Regent Street and inquired after the first available flight to Lisbon.

"Today?"

"Today, yes."

The place was crowded. There was nothing special about him, nothing particularly memorable: late bookings were happening all the time. Even so he felt safer behind dark lenses.

"This afternoon?" the girl queried, reaching for a list.

"If possible."

Her pointed fingernail came to rest halfway down a column. "Fourteen twenty-five?" She glanced at the clock, then back to Howard: it was ten minutes past twelve. "Fourteen twenty-five—or is that pushing it a bit?"

He shook his head. "Suits me."

She lifted a telephone, half turning from him as she spoke, tapping a pencil on the desk. The wait seemed endless, but eventually she said something he couldn't catch and hung up. "That'll be okay," she told him. Relief dragged at one side of his mouth. "Your name, please?"

"Elliott." It came pat. "Bruce Elliott."

"D'you want to make your return reservation now, Mr. Elliott?"

"No, I'll leave it."

She made out the ticket. "If you're taking the coach from the Cromwell Road terminal you'll need to be there within the hour."

"Thanks."

Her smile was fleeting. He paid and left. How small the world was; he'd be in Lisbon before she finished for the day. Nowhere was safe any more, no one. It cut both ways. "Macerda or Marceda; it's one of the two"— the memory stupefied him still. He crossed the road and waited between the bus stops for a cab, tumult inside his head, thinking with disbelief what his ultimate intention was, somehow separated from the meanings of things as they had once been.

He was at the terminal on the half hour. "No baggage, sir?"—it sounded like an accusation. He bought a newspaper and a couple of paperbacks, though not to read; to be empty-handed made him feel conspicuous and at all costs he didn't want to be that. He sat alone in the coach and tried to wrap his temporary self around him, bracing his nerves in readiness for immigration at Heathrow. But, in the event, he needn't have bothered: a brief glance, a nod, and he was allowed through. Ordinariness was all around, the coming nightmare within. In the hot used air of the waiting area he drank a double brandy and bought a pocket-sized bottle, duty free. When his flight number was called he descended the covered ramp in the middle of a straggling throng of fellow passengers, keeping them close, as if their apparent security and contentment offered him protection. The plane was far from full and he chose a seat just aft of the starboard wing. Once again he was spared an immediate neighbor. He buckled himself in and crushed his cigarette and, after a little while, watched without interest as the runway blurred and fell away beneath the engine pods.

2

Macerda filled every cranny of his mind. He had reckoned without Macerda. A week ago he had assured himself that his past had no loose ends, but he had overlooked the blue-chinned Portuguese. Until yesterday —only yesterday—Macerda had seemed as good as dead, harmless, an unpleasant memory: now he must be physically exterminated. There was no alternative. To outbid Shelley would be lunacy; the menace would exist as long as the man lived. But the killing of him, the actual ways and means of it, remained an unthinkable detail: Howard's mind turned squeamish once it moved in that direction. He had been close to death himself and witness to the death of others, but long ago. In desperation he sought to rid himself of the image of his quarry for a space of time, but it proved impossible. From minute to minute, from the first hour into the second, Macerda traveled with him—the greasy black hair and the cheap, scuffed, pointed shoes, the catlike springy shuffle and furtive hands and narrow black boomerang moustache—"Anything, *amigo?* Anything for me?" Even the voice was unforgettable.

Howard listened to the change in the tone of the engines that marked the beginning of the descent. Passively he watched the brown and sage-green land tilt and slide across the frame of his window. Soon, between dazzling mountains of cloud, he glimpsed the coastline; then, as they circled, Lisbon was suddenly below, multicolored on the slopes above the mottled waters of the river's mouth and the sea.

Shelley was somewhere there, Shelley who would lead him to Macerda.

All at once he couldn't remain still. Four thirty-five. . . . Unthinking, he lit a cigarette and was promptly told by a stewardess to put it out.

"Sorry, sir, but the announcement has been made." He stared at her stupidly. "And you should fasten your seat belt. We're about to land."

They came in on a long, skimming approach. The wheels powered down and the aircraft's shadow raced alongside, closing in to make contact with a jolting thud. They taxied to the apron in the lee of the cement-white airport buildings; the doors opened and Howard took his turn to pass through, head buzzing with the sensation of continuing movement. In the cool and comparative dark of the arrivals lobby he presented the passport with affected calm. Good muscular control had always been one of his assets, but it was beginning to desert him. He fidgeted, on edge as the gaunt official fingered the pages. Only a few weeks had elapsed since he was last at this barrier, and he wasn't Elliott then.

"Reason for your visit, *senhor?*"

"Business," he said.

The stamp was on the visa page almost before he realized it. He walked thankfully away, relief prickling his spine. *"Nada,"* he told the man at the customs gate.

"Tenho nada a declarar." He had hardly emerged into the clamor of the main concourse when someone touched him on the arm and he spun around as if he had been stung.

"Mr. Page?" A stranger smiled expectantly. "Mr. Page, is it?"

Howard shook his head. It suddenly struck him how vulnerable he was. Green had approached him in this area, picked him out from a planeload of others. Panic took a temporary hold; he sidled urgently through the knots of waiting people, partially shielding his face, in dread of hearing his name. Chance could finish him, here and now. He made for the exit without delay, but even the exit was too public a place. Only when he had clambered into a taxi did the fear of imminent recognition leave him.

"You want to hire a car?" the driver frowned, under way. "A self-drive car, did you say?"

"That's right."

"You could have done that in there." He jerked a thumb. "Where you came from. In the building there."

"I'll pick one up in Lisbon."

"Here would be better, surely?" They were slowing. "Not better for me, of course, but better for you. Less trouble."

"I'd rather go into Lisbon."

Their eyes met in the rearview mirror. The driver shrugged. "I will take you to the hire-car office in the Avenida da Roma. An Auto-Super office." All foreigners are fools, the shrug said.

It had gone five. The light was amber, a beautiful light that came before sundown and would last for about an hour. Unheeding, Howard let the city rattle and swerve toward him. Shelley and Macerda met at night— that much he'd discovered. But where? Gillian hadn't said, and there was a limit to what desire would yield; he'd asked all he dared of her.

The taxi swung into the forecourt of a garage. "Auto-Super," the driver said. "Auto-Super, the same as at the airport." It bothered him: he spread his hands and took his money and drove away. The office was at the rear of a line of used cars. Music throbbed from a tinny transistor and the coatless man in possession was busy manicuring his nails. A yellowing photograph of Pope John confronted a nude girl on a poster beside the desk.

Indolently the man turned the music down. *"Senhor?"* He pushed a tariff card at Howard. "The minimum period of hire is three days."

"Three days will be ample."

"For the minimum period it is the maximum rate." A printed form was pulled from a drawer. "Your passport, please."

Howard watched him record the details.

"Where will you be going, *senhor?*"

"Nowhere special."

"I am not inquisitive, *senhor*. I ask in order to tell you that you can return the car and collect your deposit at any Auto-Super office." Eyes and mouth were surly. "Now, please, your driving license."

"Driving—?"

"Please."

Christ, "I haven't got it with me."

"No?"

Howard shook his head. He felt inside his pockets, knowing nothing was there. Then he began to bluster. "I traveled at the last minute. It was a sudden decision, a matter of urgency. . . . About a villa," he said, held by the sullen stare. "It is imperative for me to have a car. Look, I've just flown in from London, and—"

"You have no license?"

"Not with me, no."

"You can hire a car with a driver. The rates are more expensive, but—"

"I want to drive myself."

The man shrugged and dropped his gaze.

"I've held a license for twenty years," Howard protested. "I forgot to bring it, that's all. I was in a hurry."

The man ran his tongue over his teeth. Otherwise he didn't move. He seemed indifferent to Howard's dilemma. A full half-minute must have gone by. Howard took a five-pound note from his pocket and placed it blatantly on the desk. "The number of my license is 6—054812."

The transistor's beat blurred a crescendo. "6—054812," Howard repeated.

"How sure are you of that?"

"One hundred percent." He lied so well.

"Where is this villa?"

"Not far—Cascais."

The note slowly crumpled in the man's fist. "6—054812?"

"Correct."

"District?"

"London."

"Date of expiry?"

"December next. December thirty-first."

The form was completed. Howard paid the deposit in sterling and signed. The man rose, selected a key from a rack and led Howard around to a space at the back of the office.

"Simca," he said, opening a jaded blue saloon. "First-class condition. One of the best self-drives on the road."

Howard took the key from him and got in. There were more than sixty thousand kilometers on the clock and practically everything shook when the engine turned over. At any other time he would have demanded something less used, but he was in no position to pick and choose; the tank was full and the battery was charging. He adjusted the seat and familiarized himself with the layout.

"Take it easy, *Senhor* Elliott," the man said. For an awful moment Howard wondered who he meant. "And remember—you had your license when you were here."

3

He let in the clutch and took to the Avenida da Roma. The gradients soon had him working up and down through the gears. He headed south, doglegging in the direction of the river, memory guiding him. The embassy was in the Lapa quarter, only a stone's throw from the waterfront at Alcantara, and he thought it possible that Shelley might still be there. Nose-to-the-grindstone Shelley. "What cars do first secretaries run to these days?" he'd tossed lightly at Gillian. "Something swish, I bet." So he knew what to look for—a fawn Rover 3500.

He glimpsed the bull ring to his right and, in the distance, the twin Romanesque towers of the cathedral. The city undulated from hill to hill, reared and twisted and leveled out, but he was oblivious of the vistas. Grim-faced, he competed with the traffic's cut and thrust. Soon he was circling into the tree-lined spaciousness of the Avenida da Liberdade. Halfway down its length he turned into the honking crisscross of streets that lay to the west of the Rossio. Within a mile he reached the Tagus at the ferry station: the choppy water had a molten glow. He swung downstream toward the huge suspension bridge and the wharves at Alcantara. He had met Macerda near the railway yards here; with sickening despair the thought intruded. A white-gloved policeman checked his progress, then let him loose along with a gaggle of other vehicles. He filtered clear of the onward rush and went with a rubbery tattoo across the cobbles into the side streets north of the docks, leaving the warehouse dust and drabness in his wake.

There wasn't a patch of this area he didn't know. He went left, then right, then left again, balconied mansions to either side, no shops, no bars, few pedestrians. He braked well short of the British embassy, slid into a vacant space by the curb and looked for Shelley's car. Among those parked immediately outside was the dark Hillman in which Green had driven him last month, but there was no Rover. Its absence didn't perturb him too much; he'd partly expected to find that Shelley had gone home. "Are you still at the same place?"—it had been only natural to inquire. Without emotion Howard gazed briefly at the embassy, with its fine entrance and filigree balconies and angled flag pole, then signaled he was pulling out and drove away. Shelley lived quite close and Howard didn't once hesitate at an intersection; he couldn't have lost his way if he'd tried. Less than five minutes after leaving the Rua San Domingos he was entering the small quiet garden square where Shelley had his flat. Again he parked at a discreet distance and again he looked for the Rover. It wasn't to be seen and this time anxiety dug deeper.

153

Shelley was his lynch-pin. Surely he wasn't already with Macerda?—not already? At night, Gillian had said. "At night, yes. He's been going out after dinner."

It was only dusk now. Howard lit a cigarette. Shelley wasn't his own master. Macerda would be calling the tune, saying where and when. In the past he had come and gone by night, but he was anything but predictable. Thoughtfully Howard blew smoke against the windscreen. He must wait where he was, wait and go on waiting, and somehow keep a hold on his imagination.

The light drained a little more out of the air. It was quiet in the square, Lisbon's traffic no more than a dyspeptic rumble. Howard was finishing his second cigarette when a car slowed alongside, braking, indicator on the wink. Shelley's. Howard stiffened, relief chopped short by the realization that the Rover was pulling into the gap directly in front of him. He sank a little lower in his seat and watched tensely as Shelley eased his long frame upright and walked diagonally away. Gillian didn't enter Howard's thinking; Geoffrey Shelley had too often been dishonored. Head turned, he saw him fade into the dusk and then, after an interval, a trio of second-floor windows light up.

Six forty: Howard checked. Had Shelley made his rendezvous? The likelihood was that he hadn't, but only time would tell. He pulled the bottle from a side pocket and drank, the brandy deadening the terror to which he was committed. He drank carefully, with measured deliberation. Night settled and the lights remained in Shelley's window. An hour later they were still there and the bottle was more than half empty. Howard grew cramped and got out of the car and walked up and down for a while. At eight thirty he was behind the wheel again, smoking the last but one cigarette of a pack he'd bought on the plane that afternoon. Time had lost its shape. Every so often he tilted the bottle against his lips, dulling what he could of himself.

Nine o'clock sounded from a nearby church. Passersby were rare: vaguely he listened to their footfalls come and go. After what seemed an age, Shelley's windows suddenly went dark. Howard sent the butt of his cigarette spinning and screwed expectantly in his seat. The square was poorly lit: Shelley was unidentifiable until he reached the Rover and ducked under the saloon's roof light. He reversed close to the Simca to give himself room and Howard allowed him perhaps fifty yards before going in pursuit. He closed the gap a little, then tagged on, determined not to lose him.

The obvious he remembered—the Estrela basilica, the Parliament building—but he could never have retraced the exact route. Where there was heavy traffic it seemed to conspire to separate them. Twice he was last across at traffic lights, accelerating to keep in touch while other drivers gestured or screamed abuse. Shelley led him through the narrow confines of the Baixa district, then backtracked toward the river. Deviousness was an elementary safeguard, yet Howard hadn't expected it of him. In places, where streets intersected in quick succession, he couldn't afford to give Shelley too long a lead, yet to stay too close was to invite suspicion. He spurted whenever the Rover turned and vanished, braked when he saw it again. The streets were little more than alleys now, peeling walls to either side, low doorways, dim lights. No tourists visited here. Seamen and soldiers came, in search of relief: they stood on the narrow pavements as Howard kept his distance behind Shelley. A radio blared, a woman laughed. There was a rancid smell, all-pervading.

Shelley stopped without warning. Howard pulled in sharply and a taxi overtook them both, squeezed for space. Shelley got out, locked the car and went through a doorway. Howard cut the engine and waited, peering forward. So this was where Macerda buried himself. He reached for the bottle, still a third full, and gulped some brandy. It must drug him more yet, help him to hate.

"You want a girl, *senhor?*" Someone stood at his elbow, someone old, lined, a woman herself.

"No." He was startled. She looked at him with pity. "No," he said fiercely. "Go away."

He drank again, eyes traveling over the windows above the door where Shelley had gone in; altogether there were three storys. A fraction remained of him that

155

was unable to believe what was going to happen; the rest knew, knew for sure, and tried to find refuge from it. He opened another pack of cigarettes and lit one, the flame shaking. How close was Macerda to being tempted? How much in money and patience separated Shelley from what he was after? Faced with his cautious inflexibility, Macerda might be driven to play his hand—not all, but sufficient to show the quality of what he had to offer. The name he would withhold to the end, but he was greedy and would therefore be eager to settle. Shelley would wear him down. Perhaps tonight. Perhaps it was too late already—"Lawrence, a naval officer called Lawrence."

Howard finished the brandy. His brain was on fire. He sat and watched the door through which Shelley would emerge. "Still waiting, *senhor?*" This time it was a girl. He shook his head and wound up the window and sweated, preparing himself. It couldn't be much longer. Shelley had been gone an hour. Which floor was it? He peered, everything slightly out of focus. A dog nosed along the muck in the gutters. Drunken voices came from one of the bars. Poverty and lust bargained softly in the warm dark. The minutes passed. He blinked sweat from his eyes and shivered inside himself. Macerda should have left well enough alone; that way he would have spared them both.

Something must have distracted him, because he didn't see Shelley actually step into the street. Suddenly he was there, crossing to the car. Howard's heart pounded, a weakness taking him in the belly. Did he know yet? Through a blur he watched Shelley get into the Rover and drive away, the rear lights vanish. Now, his mind said. An emergency tool kit lay wrapped in a corner of the parcel shelf. He drew out the large spanner and pushed it up his right sleeve, holding it there. Someone else seemed to choose the weapon for him. He left the car and went to the door Shelley had used: it was of heavy wood, banded with iron, but it moved easily. Inside was a square stone lobby where a lamp burned and a gray-haired janitor sat reading a newspaper at a table. Stairs led to the upper floors.

The janitor peered. "Yes?" He looked over the top of steel-framed spectacles. "Yes?" he asked in a dry voice.

"Does Rafael Macerda live here?"

"Number seven." The man shielded his eyes from the lamp. "Wasn't it you a minute ago—?" he began to say, but didn't finish. The frown left his face and he resumed his study of the newspaper. "Number seven," he repeated, interest gone.

Bars of shadow filled the well of the staircase: Howard moved across them like someone imprisoned. The handrail steadied him as he climbed. He walked up slowly, putting on the gloves. Four doors opened off the first landing, each of them numbered. He passed them by, a dank smell everywhere, resonance, noise coming from behind the doors—shouting, shuffling, singing. He went on up. Number five was at the top of the next flight, six and seven further along. He stopped outside number seven, dementedly trying not to believe this was him. The spanner slid down the sleeve into his right hand. He knocked on the scabrous door, standing close, ready. And when it opened—a slit only—time seemed momentarily to hold still, shock and sudden fear on the visible segment of Macerda's face.

"You." It was like a leaf rustle, drawn out, incredulous.

Howard shoved his foot in the gap as Macerda threw himself against the door. For ten seconds or so Macerda managed to hold his own; the only sound was his panting and the creak of wood. Then Howard's strength pushed him back. He abandoned the doorway and scurried across the room. There was nothing but a room—a bed, some furniture, a plastic curtain drawn on the far side; that was all. Howard closed the door with his foot.

"For the love of Christ," Macerda whispered. He'd always whispered. Now there was terror in the sibilance. "For the love of Christ."

Howard aimed the first blow at his head, but he warded it off, moving behind a chair, cringing.

"He doesn't know. He doesn't know. . . . Shelley doesn't know."

Howard caught him by the collar of his shirt and

157

crashed the spanner against Macerda's neck, below the left ear. Macerda grunted, hope still frantic in his eyes.

"I haven't told him who it was. . . . He doesn't have your name."

He was making sure of his death with every phrase. Howard struck him again—higher, twice more, three times. Blood spurted from Macerda's skull. One side of his face was a flowing tide of scarlet.

"He doesn't know it was you."

Somehow he managed to make himself clear. He was on his knees, hands grappling feebly, clutching at the spanner, succeeding in snatching it away. He fell against the curtain, ripping it from the rail. Howard stumbled, wishing himself deaf and blind. Macerda gabbled beneath the folds of plastic, moving, pleading still, words only now, incapable of sentences. There was a bath behind where the curtains had hung. Howard dragged Macerda across the floor, unable to strike him again. He picked him up and heaped him into the bath, blocked the hole and turned the taps.

"No," Macerda whimpered, revived by the rush of water. "I swear it."

He thrashed about a little, though not much. He stared up at Howard as if he were staring into the memory of some other time. Howard thrust him down and the rushing water turned to crimson, the vivid color deepening, hiding Macerda from him with obscene mercy. Great bubbles broke the surface with a gurgling noise. The body went limp. Howard turned off the taps and watched Macerda float, half submerged, air ballooning his blue shirt and gray cotton trousers.

But for the brightness of the blood he looked as if he'd been dead for days.

4

Whenever the nightmare unreeled itself Howard remembered washing in a basin set beneath a spattered mirror, dabbing his suit, wiping his shoes, rinsing and squeezing out his stained suede gloves. Sometimes he remembered cleaning the spanner, sometimes not. The after-sequence was never precisely the same, the impressions shaky and indistinct. *Not me*, he would recoil. Then, horror-stricken, the killing would begin to run slow-motion through his mind and every flimsy shred of instinctive pretense would perish.

It was *me. Oh Christ, oh God, it was me. . . .*

The last thing he heard as he left the room was the slop-slop of water in the bath. He paused at the top of the stairs, then started down, weak at the knees, the spanner hidden in his sleeve. *"You"*—Macerda's voice whispered close behind, driving him away. In trauma Howard descended into the bands of light from the janitor's lamp. *"Adeus,"* the man said absently, but Howard didn't hear. He went out into the narrow street, teeth beginning to chatter. He got in the car, unable to control his jaws. "Shelley doesn't know. . . ." A drunken sailor lurched alongside and pawed at him, wanting money. Howard flinched from the contact. He switched on and crashed into gear; the tires yelped as if in pain.

He found himself by the river, numbness thawing out of him fast. He pulled into the side and retched, but nothing came. Barges squatted under their riding lights, lovers huddled in the shadows, a cat mewed. And Macerda was dead. The sodium glow of the city dimmed the lowermost stars. Dead, soft-spoken to the last. Howard was afraid to close his eyes. He shuddered. If he once closed his eyes Macerda would show him what had happened, exactly how it was done. He could hear him as it was, feel him, smell him.

He had tossed the spanner onto the right-hand seat: a terrible effort was required to pick it up and rewrap it in the tool kit. Then, without seeming to come to any decision, he started to drive again. He must have planned earlier what he would do, where he would go. He made for the airport, enveloped by hideousness, unable to blank out his mind. Nothing registered on the way; he was never able to recall the journey. The next thing he clearly remembered was being at the Auto-Super counter on the airport's concourse. "So soon, *Senhor* Elliott?" a surprised clerk said, checking the documents.

The rigmarole of handing back the keys seemed endless. As he signed, Howard saw that his knuckles were skinned; the rawness sickened him. He walked away, reminding himself that he was safe, everything wiped clean. No one could betray him now. The muscles in his cheeks kept twitching. It was midnight. He stared at the flight departure board. There was nothing for London until midmorning, but an Air France Caravelle was leaving in forty minutes for Paris. A handful of people sat and lay on the couches in the international stand-by area. He ran past them to the Air France desk and asked if the Paris flight was fully booked. No, the brunette said after a rapid check. A single? One way? Yes, he confirmed. No baggage? No, no baggage. Ticket and passport he clasped together. There was just time before the flight was called to swallow two large brandies at the bar. For a while they helped to tranquilize his mind and dull its screaming.

A man sat beside him on the plane, a photographer, lean and flannel-suited and angry with someone for having switched his assignment. He wanted to talk about it. "One moment it's red sails on the Tagus and the next it's ye olde Montmartre. I ask you. Enough to send you round the twist."

Macerda was a thousand times more real—pleading, moaning, streaming blood. He was in Paris at three in the morning, haunting Howard in the echoing vault of the main passenger building at Orly, overlaying the natural vision as Howard waited for the early flight to London, grappling with him at seven o'clock takeoff, present at Heathrow and sharing taxis and a tube train on the way to Hampstead, lying water-logged in the bath as Howard entered the flat and, exhausted, threw himself on the bed.

Sleep was impossible. Howard chain-smoked. Bouts of shivering swept him. He should have considered a gun, a knife even. He should have thought about ways and means in advance, in detail. Others did. He should have put his mind to work, unflinching. But no. Desperation had seemed enough, that and the brandy.

God, oh God, oh God.

Over and over he told himself that he was justified, that Alex would have approved, but this didn't quieten him; Macerda remained indelible, floating swollen on the bloody water, clutching him about the knees as he was bludgeoned into extinction. Hate would have helped, but hate had failed to rise. Horror had seen to that; disgust. Even as he ran the taps and pressed Macerda down, he had been revolted.

The telephone rang—not in Lisbon, not in that nightmare room, but here, in Hampstead, now. As if dazed he lifted the receiver and cautiously spoke his name.

"Commander?"

The images scattered. "I've been ill," he explained to Miss Chancellor. "Yes. . . . No, nothing serious, An upset. I should have called you yesterday. Did you? When was that? I can only imagine I was asleep. . . . Twice?" He had no answer. "Let Captain Starey know that I expect to be at the office tomorrow, will you?"

He lit yet another cigarette, trying to piece himself together. The impromtu lie lacked conviction. He must restore his calm—the exterior calm that gained him thinking space. It was essential. He mustn't allow himself to be confused: if he became confused he thought he would go mad. Never, never at any time, was it to have been like this—Macerda murdered and Alex dead, one to terrorize him and the other perhaps to bring him down.

Perhaps. Only perhaps. What Garner lacked was proof. . . .

A block of sunlight moved imperceptibly across the wall. The hours merged and the morning passed. He kept wondering how long it would be before Macerda was found. In the street they might remember the two cars—Shelley's and his; and the janitor would remember the two men—Shelley and him. But, except for the distinctive rarity of Shelley's CD plates, no one was likely to recollect any details. Night after night there were cars in that street, all manner of cars, and men—innumerable, anonymous men. Of his own accord Shelley would come forward when the news broke: he would have no choice. In any case he would want to know what the police could tell him in addition to the cause of Macerda's death and the nature of his injuries. Not that he would learn much. It wasn't uncommon for men like Macerda, who lived

161

close to the gutter and by their wits, to reach a violent end. Questions would remain, and Shelley would curse himself for having haggled once too often. But nowhere in his thinking would there be the remotest possibility of a connection between what had happened and Gillian's visit to London.

Howard roused himself and made coffee. He couldn't eat; he seemed to have lost the need for food. Macerda came at him like a ghost and he managed to shake him off. Gillian would be back in Lisbon now. He thought of her distractedly. Everything was telescoped, time and place and action. But for her Macerda would still be alive—and there were moments when he almost wished he was.

The bell rang. He swung his legs off the bed and went lightheaded to the door.

"Good afternoon, commander. May I come in?"

His scalp seemed to shrink. It was Garner.

CHAPTER FOUR

1

"I understand from Captain Starey that you're a bit off-color, so I won't detain you long. But there are one or two things I need to ask, and I'd rather get shot of them during office hours." Garner brought his mirthless smile to bear. "It's my wife's birthday and we're dining out."

"What d'you want to know?"

"In particular I'd like to refresh my memory about something I put to you when we first met."

"Very well." Howard used all his technique to gain a

little time. "D'you mind if I sit down? Lousy thing, this. Some sort of bug. It knocked me sideways yesterday."

"What does your doctor say?"

"I haven't bothered him. I'll be all right by tomorrow." He rubbed his beard-stubble, mind in tatters, the casual veneer desperately thin, warning himself that part of Garner's skill was to seem to be harmless. "Forgive my appearance. . . . Cigarette?"

"I don't thanks." With slight disdain Garner's wet blue eyes watched him light up. "When I was here before, commander, I asked you whether you possessed a type-writer."

"That's right."

"You remember?"

"Oh yes."

"And you said you did not."

Howard nodded. "That's right."

"I wondered how positive you were about that."

"If I told you I haven't got a typewriter then I haven't got one."

Garner fingered his trouser creases. He must have known he'd be stone-walled. "Has that always been the case?"

"For years it has."

"When was the last time?"

"Offhand I can't recall." Howard narrowed his should-ers. "Six or seven years."

"Not since?"

"No."

"Not during your time in this flat?"

"No."

"If someone were to state otherwise, what would you say?"

"I would say she's mistaken."

"She?" Garner flashed. "She, commander?" He let the question hang there, challenging Howard to hold his gaze. The pause seemed endless. "She would be lying, would she?"

"Mistaken."

"What a difference a word makes." The empty smile

163

was like a threat. "Perhaps I'm misleading you by harping on ownership. Maybe you've had a typewriter on hire?"

"No."

"On loan?"

"No."

Hours ago Howard had thrown his jacket over the chair beside the one in which Garner was sitting. Suddenly, as he blew a defiant jet of smoke, he noticed the top of the Elliott passport jutting from an outer pocket. His expression changed. With undisguised alarm he rose to his feet and put the jacket on.

"Never?"

"No," he said. "Never."

Sweat prickled his skin. His heart thudded. Garner missed so little. He'd wrong-footed him already. We know a lot, his eyes said—not merely about the girl upstairs. Give us time and we'll unearth all we need. . . . Howard ground his cigarette in the tray. The nightmare hovered in the background. His wits were overstretched and he couldn't trust himself.

"I don't know anything about a typewriter," he snapped nervously, "and I'm sick of being pestered."

Garner dusted a speck from his sleeve. "It's very understandable." For half a second Howard thought he was going to get up, but he merely crossed his legs. "What golf ball do you use, commander?" He slipped it in.

"The Paxton."

"Paxton Special?"

"Yes." Too late Howard saw the danger. "Not always. Recently I—"

"Our Russian friend had a Paxton on him."

"So?"

"It's not a common make. Only four percent of the market."

"I don't always use it."

"Brogan says you do."

"He's wrong."

"Mistaken-wrong or liar-wrong?"

"Mistaken."

"Is it a habit of yours to have dealings with unreliable people?" Garner didn't wait. "That day at Burdean, the one we're talking about—where were you when the lightning struck?"

"I told you."

"Tell me again."

He varied his pace but he didn't ease up. For half an hour he kept Howard blundering from one answer to another. A few minutes more and he would have had him on the run, but he chose to leave. "Thank you, commander. . . . I don't think I need bother you any more today." He sounded almost apologetic, what appeared to be concern on his face. "I'm sorry you're so low." At the door, where he delayed before leaving, it was as if he was speaking about someone else. "It's rash to guess, but I suppose you sliced your ball into the pines, Donskoy picked it up and you forgot to ask him for it back. . . . Would that be about it, I wonder?"

He turned away. Howard pushed the door to and shut his eyes. With his forehead against a wall he listened to the faint hum of the lift. He was beginning to come apart. He couldn't think properly. Garner wasn't poking around at a few suspicions anymore; he was dealing in certainties. Everything was beginning to close in.

Howard swayed. His mouth was bone dry and there were lights exploding in the convulsions of his mind. He couldn't remember exactly what he had said, yet Garner would return another time to harass him with it, confuse him, trap him. He went into the living room. His hands felt clammy. "Your ball nearly killed me—rat-tat-tat from tree to tree"—nothing had gone right since Alex died. Garner would undermine him, wear him down. There was an inevitability about it. "Jesus," Howard breathed, staring into himself, confidence gone. An end was on its way.

He looked at the thin pink scabs which glazed his knuckles, appalled to realize that Garner had been going to manage without Macerda anyway.

BOOK FIVE

CHAPTER ONE

1

Sometimes, Daniel Somerset thought, Richard's eyes carried in them a reflection of vast areas of explored grief. *On the whole,* he wrote to the bishop's secretary, *he has settled in here very well. Naturally, it is difficult for him. The tempo is quite different from what he has been used to, and so is the scale of things. It was, of course, a great relief to him to know that his priesthood is not in jeopardy, but he finds the restrictions placed upon him irksome and quite clearly longs for a more active participation in events. Such an attitude, I would have thought, is inevitable—and characteristic. By nature he is impulsive and he tends to oversimplification. Change—as far as the church is concerned—he regards as essential. On the major issues he is, without doubt, progressive in his thinking, and I sometimes detect an impatience with those whose views differ from his. At most of the decisive moments in his life he seems to have been governed by his heart and not by his head, and he has indicated to me, in as many words, that he believes this is how the church should act also—out of an instinctive compassion that is as immediate as a reflex action. Who am I to tell him how praiseworthy such a view is, and yet, given the contemporary complexities, how impossible? He must settle for second best; most of us have along the way.*

I hope it will not be long before permission is granted for him to widen his activities: he remarks at times on the frustrations of being a partial priest. On top of every-

166

thing his old mother's health is causing concern and this has further unsettled him. Even so, I am delighted in him as a man and could not wish for a better curate. . . .

2

"Well?"

Dr. O'Sullivan tightened his lips. "I'm not too happy about her."

"A month ago you were fairly encouraging."

"A month ago there was no reason to be otherwise. Organically there's still nothing much wrong. It's *anno Domini* more than anything. The machinery's begun to run down."

"She's only in her early seventies."

"It has to start sometime." O'Sullivan looked at Richard: priests had so much experience of death that he sometimes forgot they weren't medically qualified. "And some machinery is better than others." He frowned. "This last year or so she's been inclined to make an invalid of herself—keeping to her room, taking to her bed, that kind of thing. If I may say so, I think this was perhaps to draw attention to herself as much as anything. You know your mother, Richard. But what's happening now is altogether different, and I grant you it's as sudden as it's unexpected. Still, nothing's imminent, and she's in no pain, which is a blessing."

Richard stopped: they were on the stairs. "Could my coming back have had anything to do with it? I remember being surprised to see how frail she was. She was distressed about my arm, and—"

"My dear fellow, that's the last notion you should let loose on yourself." Without meaning to, O'Sullivan's hand touched the empty sleeve. "How long are you going to be here?"

"Only an hour or so. I have to be in Evensham by late afternoon. There's a train around four."

They went on down to the hall, where O'Sullivan retrieved his hat.

"I said nothing's imminent, by which I mean that I'm thinking in terms of weeks as opposed to days. I could be

167

mistáken, of course. But, right or wrong, I feel she ought to have a nurse—at night, anyway. Mrs. Wood's a sensible, practical woman, but she can't be expected to be at your mother's beck and call twenty-four hours a day. The thing is, Richard, nurses aren't cheap." He hesitated delicately. "In view of the Wyndhams has gone downhill in recent times, I wondered—"

"There's no problem," Richard said. "If she needs a nurse she must have one, and that's that. Howard and I will underwrite the cost, don't worry."

O'Sullivan nodded. "When will you be here again?"

"Whenever I get the chance. I can't say for sure."

"What about Howard?"

"I don't know. I haven't seen him for some time, or even managed to make contact. I'll try again this evening."

They exchanged good-byes and Richard watched the Humber purr from sight behind the straggling rhododendrons. He returned inside and went slowly up the stairs to Tibbie's room.

"I heard a car," she said.

"O'Sullivan was leaving."

"Oh." It was a sigh. "What did he tell you?"

"He's arranging for you to have a nurse, mother."

"A nurse?"

"At night."

"Why?"

"He thinks it best. And so do I. It's only fair on Mrs. Wood."

A bird fluttered the ivy close to the open window. "What else did O'Sullivan say?"

"That you're tired. Very, very tired."

"Is that all?"

"Yes."

"Tired," she said, as if listening to the sound of the word. Then: "He should have spoken to me about the nurse."

"He will, mother."

"First, I mean. I may not like her."

"In which case we'll get someone you do."

"I'm too old to be fussed by strangers. Not that it matters, I suppose."

The voice was a murmur, the eyes sunken and sluggish, the shriveled face almost aquiline. Only the dulling mercy of the years could have made her so indifferent.

"Tell Father Wyatt I wish to see him, will you?"

"Of course."

He felt no slight: it was unimaginable that she should confess to him. She drifted into sleep and he looked at her with pity, sad at her friendlessness. He stayed for a while, first at the bedside and then at the window, gazing out at the tangled ruin of what was once an ordered garden. "Shall I tell you something?" he remembered his father saying with hopeless venom. "It's an equation: affection equals heartache. Give one, get the other. It stands to reason. The more we give it the more the heartache will finally be, yet like fools we go on giving. Not your mother, though. She'll be spared any of that; she'll be lonely instead. . . ." He wasn't often disloyal, Richard reflected, but once in a while he had been shrewdly prophetic.

Toward half past three he tiptoed from the room and walked downstairs. In the hall he telephoned for a taxi, then went into the kitchen.

"I'm catching the four o'clock, Mrs. Wood, so I'll be off in a few minutes. There's something you should know. Dr. O'Sullivan reckons Mrs. Lawrence needs a regular night nurse, so I expect by tomorrow you'll have one descend on you."

"I can't say, I'm sorry, Mr. Richard. I haven't been easy about her for several days now. In fact, I spoke to the doctor last time he called."

"Perhaps we should have thought of this earlier. It's meant a lot of extra responsibility and worry for you alone with her here."

"How bad is she, Mr. Richard?"

"Pretty bad," he admitted. "If she shows signs of getting worse, call me immediately. Meanwhile I'm going to have a word with Father Wyatt to ask him to look in, and I also hope to let my brother know the position, so you might very well have him arriving."

"Someone was inquiring after Mr. Howard only to-day."

"Where?"

"Here."

"Who was it, d'you know?"

"He didn't say."

"From the golf club, most likely."

"He didn't look like a golfer to me—not that I'm any judge."

The doorbell shrilled.

"If Mr. Howard *does* come," Mrs. Wood said, going with Richard into the hall, "shall I ask him to get in touch with you?"

"Please."

It was galling to be dependent on public transport, but the train ran to time and he was in Evensham in a little over an hour. Tibbie filled his mind on the way: until he returned from Lisbon she had always seemed so indestructible. He walked from the station to the presbytery, where he found a note from Daniel Somerset propped on the table inside the front door. *Would you please take confessions for me this evening—six to six thirty. Urgent call from the Parkers.*

It was the housekeeper's free day, and Richard made himself tea. Ten minutes before he was about to cross to the church the telephone rang.

"Richard?"

"Yes."

"Jessica."

"Why, hallo. What—?"

"I wondered if by any chance you had any knowledge of Howard's whereabouts. Don't jump to conclusions; I'm not exactly aching to see him or anything as stupid as that, but Clare's birthday was at the end of last week and, give Howard his due, I've never known him forget."

"I can't help, I'm afraid. I've called him myself several times without success."

"The office said he was away sick."

"Oh?"

"Yesterday, that was."

"News to me."

170

"I thought he might have gone to earth at Wyndhams. I tossed up whether to ring there direct or not."

"I've just come back," Richard said. "You'd have drawn a blank."

"In that case I think I'll give up the chase. I never had much enthusiasm for it, anyway." She laughed dryly. "How are you, Richard?"

"Not so bad."

"You sound more like yourself. . . . And Tibbie?"

"She's on a downward slope, I'm afraid."

"Oh God," she said.

Promptly at six he entered the church. No one was there. The aroma of incense hung on the stillness, enveloping him. There were two confessionals, Daniel Somerset's name on one, his on the other. He knelt and prayed, alone in the silence and a darkness of his own making. After a time he sat and waited, not in the box but at the end of a pew, staring down the length of the church where a few candles burned like buds on the rack near the side altar and Christ hung twisted in agony on the cross above the chancel steps. Abaguma returned to fill his mind—the sour sopping stench and the violent concussive flash, the open-sided empty church and the burning hospital huts, "fa-da, fa-da" and the screams, what he remembered and what he imagined fused together. "I'm going south, sister. . . ." The decision would nag him forever: it had proved an end and a beginning. But of what?

For twenty minutes no one broke his vigil. Eventually he heard the door groan on its hinges. He rose at once and went to the confessional, took the stole from the seat, kissed it and flipped it over his shoulders.

"Richard."

Astonished, he glanced up sharply. Howard was standing there. The light wasn't good and it didn't register how ill he looked; not at first. In his surprise all Richard could think to say was: "Is it about Tibbie?"

"No." Howard shook his head.

"What, then?"

"I have to speak to you."

"Here?"

"If I must."

"What about?"

"Me."

CHAPTER TWO

1

"You?"

"Me, yes." The voice was thick with urgency.

"All right, then."

"It's confidential."

"Of course."

"I want your word you'll keep it to yourself. Absolutely to yourself."

"Very well."

"I've got to talk with someone."

Howard moved closer and Richard was suddenly aware of the desperation in his blue and bloodshot eyes. "What is it?"

Howard hesitated, as if he had forgotten what trust was. A muscle in his cheek was twitching.

With disbelief Richard asked: "D'you want to confess?"

"Confess? No." Howard shook his head. "Not in the way you mean, not in there."

"How, then?"

"There's something I have to tell you."

"Go ahead."

"Not as a priest."

"All right."

"I've killed a man."

"You've *what?*"

"Killed a man."

172

Richard's voice was in the upper register. *"You?"*

"Yes."

"When?"

"Three days ago."

"What happened?" An accident; it could only have been an accident.

"I murdered him," Howard said.

For an appalled moment Richard did not move. Then, abruptly, he got up, walked to the door and slid the bolts across. Coming back, he said: "Where was this?"

"In Lisbon."

"Lisbon? Three days ago?" With an air of stunned stupidity Richard repeated himself. "You were in Lisbon three days ago?"

"Yes."

"Why?"

"Because that's where he was." Howard faltered. To Richard he seemed to be speaking through the nausea of some awful unreality. "I can't get him out of my mind. I never thought—"

"Who was he?"

"He . . . he would have shopped me. He was on the point of it."

"Blackmail?"

"No."

"You've got to explain."

"He was once a contact of mine. A go-between."

"I don't understand."

Howard's fingers struggled with each other. "He knew about me."

"In what way?"

"I thought if I silenced him—"

"You aren't answering the questions. What did he know about you?"

"Enough."

"Tell me."

Howard seemed deaf when it suited him. Wild-eyed he said: "I'd forgotten he was left-handed. At one point he got the spanner away."

"Do you mean—?"

"Half the time he kept saying 'For the love of Christ.'

173

Even after I started hitting him he went on at it." Howard sucked in air with a shudder. "And it was all for nothing. It needn't have happened. Garner's practically sewn me up as it is."

"Garner?"

Howard nodded impatiently, as if Richard should have know.

"Listen," Richard said. "You're going to have to tell me chronologically—A to Z. Otherwise I'm lost. Who's Garner?" He waited, swamped by a sense of irrecoverable disaster. "What's Garner to do with this other man?"

"Nothing. Not directly."

"Is that meant to help?" Richard's tone hardened. "Howard—for God's sake. What d'you expect of me?"

"Patience."

"And?"

"You gave your word."

"It doesn't bind me." He was filled with a terrible desire to protect. "Confession would."

"I told you—no."

"Doesn't it mean anything?"

Howard shook his head.

"I wouldn't have thought you'd have had the guts to say that."

"Richard—"

"Begin at the beginning."

"Macerda wasn't a beginning. He was a stepping-stone, someone along the way."

"Is this the person you say you killed?"

Howard lowered his gaze. "There's only one beginning."

"Is he the man?" Richard persisted.

"Yes." A spluttering candle lapped the intensity of the silence. "He wouldn't go down. I couldn't finish him except in the bath, and when I ran the water—" Howard broke off. "I'm living with it, Richard. Day and night. There's nobody else I could speak to. Only you. I felt that if I got it out of myself it might somehow—"

"What was it he knew about you?"

"I told you—he was once my Lisbon contact."

"Contact with whom?"

174

"The Russians."

For a long moment it didn't sink in. "How—?" Richard began, then stopped, incredulity slowly molding his features. The pause seemed endless. With bewildered pedantry he finally said: "Are you saying what I believe you're saying?"

"Yes."

"You worked for them?"

"I still do."

"Nonsense." He had reached the limit of rejection.

"It isn't nonsense." Howard ran both hands over his face. In a flat voice he said: "Now you've had the second barrel; but you'd have known about it soon enough. The headlines aren't all that far off. A lot of luck's gone Garner's way, and—"

"Garner?"

"Special Branch."

Richard couldn't believe his own calmness.

"I'm getting out," Howard was saying. "But I had to see you, I had to talk about Macerda. I was half cut—deliberately—but it didn't help. All I knew was that if I was going to survive he would have to be eliminated. Right up to the last I shut my mind to how I'd do it." A haunted look was in his eyes. "I can't tell you how often I had to hit him. I took the spanner from the car. He never shouted; he just whispered at me. It went on and on. And when I held him under the water it seemed as if he was drowning in his own blood. . . . He's never left me since then. I can't shake him off."

For the third or fourth time someone rattled the latch on the door. Richard hesitated: finally he crossed behind the pews and opened up. A woman in a headscarf was standing on the steps.

"Am I too late, father?"

"No," he said mechanically, in a daze. "No, of course not."

He went into the box. Howard had moved away. The woman came and knelt at the grille and Richard listened to the trifles of her conscience, only half listening to a voice with a person on the dark end of it, murder and treachery trampling the shocked threshold of his mind.

Presently he found himself addressing the woman: "Say three Our Fathers, and mean every word. And pray for all those who live in torment." He absolved her in a monotone.

"God bless you, father."

She lit a candle from one which waned; nothing lasted. Richard's thoughts spun in the chaos of anguish and despair. Howard was slowly pacing the far aisle—a stranger suddenly, an unknown quantity; the realization was chilling. The woman genuflected and walked out of the church, the clack of her heels brisk and confident. Richard shot the bolts a second time; it was twenty to seven. Howard approached again, gaunt and garrulous.

"I'd have gone mad if I hadn't been able to talk with you. There's no one else."

"Don't you have friends?" Richard said sharply. "How long have you worked for them?"

"Twenty years."

"And there's no one—no one you could confide in?" It would have been easy to scoff. "After all that time?"

"There was," Howard said, and the emptiness in his voice fluttered from wall to wall. "There was, but there isn't now."

"So you had to come to me?"

"About Lisbon, yes."

"The dead diminish." It was meant as a kindness. The compound at Abaguma, the airfield at Kasfareet—both were indelible. Richard glanced at Howard; horror would stay with him as long as consciousness lasted. He heard himself to say: "What's this about getting out? Where will you go?"

"Beyond reach."

"You realize Tibbie's ill?"

"My staying wouldn't help either of us."

"What about the girls? Jessica called me this afternoon. Clare's birthday was—" It sounded absurd: Richard dried, swept anew by the enormity of Howard's disclosures. "How did this start?" The newspaper phrases eluded him. "What turned you, for God's sake?" He groped for a reason. "Korea, was it? When you were a prisoner?"

"Korea helped."

176

"Only helped?"

"I doubt if I could explain."

"You've been a great explainer in your time."

"I've needed to be."

"Then the truth shouldn't be too difficult."

"I wasn't granted a blinding flash like you," Howard snapped defiantly. "We don't all take the Damascus road."

"But treason. . . . To betray one's country—"

"You make it sound shameful."

"Isn't it?"

"Not necessarily."

"Not even for a serving officer?"

"One can betray more important things. Most people do. I have."

"Such as?"

"Ask Jessica."

If it was cant it was superbly camouflaged. Their eyes met, but Howard's shied away.

"And I've killed a man. . . . Which is worse, for Christ's sake—that, or the transfer of information?"

"You make it sound innocuous." Richard paused, juggling pity and contempt. "What hooked you?" he asked relentlessly. "Korea apart, what was it? You, of all people," he added, and it was as if their father had phrased the complaint, the military ethos resurrected.

"You'd never understand."

"I can try."

A muscle flicked in Howard's cheek. "This isn't why I'm here. I'm scared, Richard."

"There's always a price to pay." A moth fluttered past. "Are you so certain of a welcome mat? What happens if they don't want to know?"

"I've served them long enough."

"So you say. But why? For what reason? Don't tell me you're ideologically committed. Not you. Don't tell me you've been working for the shape of things to come." Richard swung on his heels. A bus growled in the street, but the commonplace had never seemed so remote. "How valuable are you?" He didn't wait to be answered. "What's it been—quantity or quality?"

"Listen—"

"God help you when you've exhausted your usefulness. It runs out fast these days."

"I'll be all right."

"Like now, I suppose? Like now, when there's no one to come to but me."

Howard moved his hands in protest.

"What did you ever get from them?"

"Respect."

"In Lisbon?"

"Everywhere but there."

"Respect?"

"Yes."

"Praise? Appreciation?"

"Yes." He said it as if he'd found a faith.

So that was the key. "What was Macerda in it for?"

"Money."

There was the Howard whose eyes forever moved as he talked or listened, forever questioned: do I please you—impress you?—intrigue you? . . . Women fell for that one. And there was another whose tongue was sharp with derision and resentment, whose career was run-of-the-mill in a service that had never accepted him at his own valuation.

"Money," he repeated with disdain.

Richard straightened slowly. For some reason he chose that moment to say: "It will be impossible to shield the children—d'you realize that? They'll be the worst sufferers; at school, for instance. Kids can be awful to each other."

"Keep Lisbon from them." Howard fixed him nervously with his bloodshot stare. "From Tibbie, Jessica . . . everyone. That's all I ask."

"All!"

"You talk a lot about mercy."

"You're playing with words, and you know it." Richard fingered the stole. Even if Howard had knelt in the box he would have suspected his motive; deceit was like a drug.

"No one will connect me with what happened. The records will show that I was never out of England. Garner

178

has taken my passport." Cunning emerged like a wraith. "I traveled—"

"Don't tell me," Richard warned. "You may regret it."

"I want you to see I'm not asking for myself. I won't be around."

"Isn't it late in the day to start considering others?"

"I didn't make a career out of it, like you," Howard countered, hands never still. "Richard," he said. "Richard, for God's sake. I'll be gone after tonight. You couldn't stop me, even if you wanted to."

The light was draining away. Richard moved further along the aisle toward the side altar. Impossibly, his left arm ached; the sense of loss stirred in him like an awareness of exile. Without expecting a reply he said: "Discontent produces disastrous converts." He thought of Wyndhams in a fleeting compression of images, and then of Howard's "I hate this place." He said: "What was uppermost in your mind? Revenge, was it? Some kind of revenge?"

"I had my reasons."

"Based on need or conviction?"

"You'll have to be less clever."

"Surely not."

Howard licked his lips. "Alex once said to me—"

"Alex?"

"Alex was a friend. If he were alive I wouldn't be here tonight."

Suddenly he began to speak of Garner again, Garner and a Paxton, Garner and the sixth at Burdean, a distraught torrent of words which Richard could neither stem nor follow. They neither of them heard the yawning creak of the vestry door. "Ah—there you are." It spun them around, this third voice in the cavernous silence where only theirs had been. "Is anything wrong, father?" Daniel Somerset.

"Wrong? No."

"It's well after time, and I wondered—" He caught sight of Howard and stopped short. "I'm so sorry. I had no idea."

179

Richard said clumsily. "My brother . . . I don't think you've met . . . Father Daniel Somerset."

With a kind of alarm he watched them shake hands. Already it was in his mind that Daniel would one day raise his busy eyebrows and ask: "Was that him—that night in the church?"

"I didn't mean to interrupt. Please forgive me."

"Not at all," Howard said. "I was on the point of going, anyway."

He had somehow excavated another version of himself—instantly calm, under control.

"Must you?" Richard said urgently. "Why not come over to the house?"

"Thanks all the same, but not tonight. Some other time."

Everything about him was a lie, a corruption, an exercise in survival: Richard could see it now. Yet, appalled, he glimpsed a terrible immaturity. He wanted to say: "How can you possibly go like this? You haven't so much as begun to explain. You owe it to yourself to stay. To me, to everyone. If you go now it's good-bye, finish." But Daniel was there, beaming, gagging him. He gestured distractedly. "Just for a few minutes? . . . One for the road?"

"I'm sorry."

They moved past the guttering candles. *What good's it done you to come?* Richard thought in a fever. *You can never have yourself back as you once were. I can't shift responsibility. . . . When the headlines start what would you have me explain to those who thought they knew you? . . .*

There were a hundred things to ask, to be said; a thousand. They stepped out into the dusk and walked between the gravestones to the gate and the evening's traffic.

"Where—?" Richard began, and Howard saw the question coming.

"I don't know. Somewhere to lick my wounds. . . . Good-bye, father." He nodded formally. " 'Bye, Richard." For a moment it seemed as though he might say more, but he suddenly turned and left them as if he feared his calm was beyond sustaining.

"That's really a surprise," Daniel Somerset remarked as the dusk covered Howard over. "I wasn't aware you had a brother."

2

Night-long the shock renewed itself. The cocks crowed early, but dawn was slow to come. When he looked at himself in the bathroom mirror next morning, Richard's eyes were bruised from lack of sleep. Years seemed to have passed through his brain. He felt numb, leaden, no tumult gathered in him, only an immeasurable sadness for a ruined life.

Disbelief had withered within seconds of Howard's first opening his mouth. It was true, all of it, everything. MISSING NAVAL OFFICER . . . The coming news scares could wait. Night-long, over and over, he listened to his memory of Howard unburdening himself; night-long and day-long the teeming questions remained and the bleak fact weighed him down. He took them into the weekend with him, alone with them, inescapably troubled by a sense of doom. He glossed over the Sunday features on Biafra; Uli and Enugu and Owerri were like reminders of another existence. "How much easier it is," Howard had once said, "to love those who aren't close to you." There was nothing about Howard, though, not a word.

On the Wednesday Mrs. Wood telephoned and Richard flung a few things into a grip and caught a train to Marsden.

"How long d'you give her now?"

"Perhaps a few days." O'Sullivan's estimates weren't impressive; a week had already proved him wrong. Time was shrinking. John Wyatt had administered the last rites. Tibbie lay propped on the pillows like a doll, her veined hands as cold as marble, her breathing so shallow that it was sometimes difficult to realize that she lived.

"I'll see myself out." O'Sullivan puckered his nose condescendingly. "Don't bother to come down."

Mrs. Wood sat knitting in the chair at the end of the bed. Richard crossed the room. "When did Mrs. Lawrence say she'd be here?" He was talking about Jessica.

181

"As near to seven as she can manage. She's leaving the children with her parents, so she's got a roundabout journey."

Tibbie made a sound. Richard bent over her. Her eyelids fluttered.

"Howard?"

"It's Richard, mother. Richard."

"Where's . . . Howard?"

"He'll be coming."

"When?"

"Soon," he said to placate her. "Soon now."

He exchanged glances with Mrs. Wood. What would have happened, he wondered in despair, if Howard had been able to forgive Tibbie her strength and their father his pride? It was futile to speculate and he winced the notion away. Obsessively she asked for no one but Howard, feebly seeking even now the unflagging charm and flattery. Irony had no end.

He beckoned to Mrs. Wood to join him by the window. "When did this start?"

"Yesterday." They whispered.

"The same as now?"

"I'd say she's a shade more fretful today. . . . Such a shame, Mr. Richard. He was always so kind to her, always. She looked forward to his coming."

Clouds had shuttered the sun. A soft, almost imperceptible rain set in. The nurse arrived at six, a slight, dark-haired, brisk-mannered woman. She said to Richard: "I really think there ought to be a day nurse for her now."

"There will be as from tomorrow. It's arranged."

She busied about with professional thoroughness. "May I ask you to leave?" she requested, bringing in towels and twitching the curtains. "I'll let you know when she's ready again."

"Howard? Is that Howard?"

"Richard, mother."

"Are you still on about that son of yours?" the nurse said, singsong as if to a child.

Richard went downstairs with Mrs. Wood. "Thanks so much for all you've done. I'm more than grateful."

"She's stubborn, you know, Mr. Richard."

He nodded.

"She won't let go without Mr. Howard getting here. Where *can* he be, d'you imagine?"

He went into the study and poured himself a scotch, pain frozen into his heart. He knew too much, yet not enough; nowhere near. He listened to the small sounds and the great silence of the old house and told himself he remembered laughter. Shortly before seven Jessica's Mini grated to a standstill on the drive and he hurried outside. Jessica's ease of manner was habitual; she wore it like an armor against further disillusion. Life, her appearance proclaimed, had no surprises left.

"How is she?"

Richard kissed her on the cheek. "Come and see."

"Is Howard here?"

"No."

"But that's ridiculous."

The truth would embroil her before long. He teetered on the brink of letting her share most of it with him, but he could not, at least not then. Shame, was it? He wasn't certain he felt shame. There was so much he wasn't certain of yet; only that Howard had been lost and undeniably afraid. Shame? He shook the thought away. There were other things.

"Will you have a drink? Gin or something?"

"Not at the moment. About Howard—"

Richard said quickly: "I haven't been able to contact him."

"You, too?"

Mrs. Wood put her head around the door. "Nurse says it's quite all right for you to go up now."

Tibbie's skin shone, taut and transparent across the sharp white bones. "It's Jessica, mother."

"Jessica?"

"Hallo, Tibbie dear."

"Where's Howard?" The dry lips quivered: she had dominated for so long. She opened her eyes and gazed about her with a trace of panic. To Jessica she said: "Have you brought him with you?" It used to happen.

"Not this time, Tibbie."

Jessica motioned Richard aside. "Is he on leave, or

what? The DNI told me he was sick, but that was a few days ago. When did you try the office last?"

He stalled: "They haven't a clue where he is."

Tibbie's fingers were beating a tattoo on the embroidered hem of the sheet. "I want Howard. I want . . . him here."

Jessica said to Richard through her poise, "If only we knew who, we might know where." There was a time when it would have cost her something to admit that. She trapped Richard's sidelong glance with a bitter smirk. "Don't tell me you imagine he's alone?"

"I do, yes."

"Howard?"

"Yes."

He had never been on surer ground. And there was suddenly more in his mind than a single certainty. All at once there was an idea, a blind guess, that grew the longer it possessed him, grew and made increasing sense. Steyrhofen. . . .

Was it possible? He turned his back impulsively on Tibbie and the frenetic intensity of her demands. "You're sedating her, surely?" Jessica was asking the nurse. Steyrhofen—"the best time we ever shared, remember?" Was it so ridiculous to suppose Howard might have headed there? "Beyond reach," he'd said with shaky bravado. Steyrhofen was anything but that, but the borders were close by, the dubious welcome and the new loneliness. "Don't you have friends?" the question had been and the empty answer had shown itself in Howard's eyes. He would hesitate before taking the final plunge.

"Excuse me a moment."

Richard left the room and hurried down to the study and the telephone. There was a Lufthansa flight, Heathrow to Klagenfurt, in three hours' time. A kind of inevitability had begun to take hold of him. Steyrhofen? "Somewhere to lick my wounds. . . ." It was a chance in a thousand, yet instinct insisted that Richard didn't let it go to waste. He stared out at the drizzle, thoughts racing. His new passport was in the house. Seven to eight hours would see him there. If it were all a madness, and he was wrong, he could be back at Tibbie's bedside by tomorrow afternoon. And if it wasn't . . . ? The headlong rush faltered. He thought of Garner; there was more to this than a guessing game.

He chewed his lower lip, picturing the village and its one hotel, its one church and its two streets. Howard wouldn't be difficult to find, no matter what name he'd assumed.

And yet. . . .

He wavered. He went back upstairs, going quietly into the room. Jessica must have heard him using the phone. "Were you trying the flat?"

"No."

"Who is it?" Tibbie peered, hope like a lifeline.

"Richard, mother."

"I want Howard," she breathed. The world was retreating and her insistence was pathetic. "Tell Howard to come."

He looked at her hopelessly.

"Please. . . ."

"I'll do what I can," he said in desperation, indecision suddenly at an end. He bent and kissed the pale forehead. "He's away, you see. But I think I know where I can reach him."

"There now, Mrs. Lawrence," the nurse declaimed, "everything's going to be fine."

Jessica was at the door. "Was that the wisest thing to tell her?" she challenged Richard.

"It's a gamble, but at most I'll only be gone twenty-four hours."

She frowned, lips parted. "D'you mean you're actually going somewhere?"

"Yes."

"Where?"

"Austria."

She was astonished beyond concealment. "He's in Austria? . . . Howard?"

"Perhaps."

"Only perhaps? And on the strength of a perhaps you're—"

"Steyrhofen, not far from Klagenfurt."

"Has he left word, or something?" She could only have been thinking about the phone call.

He shook his head. "It's a shot in the dark, Jessica."

"You must be crazy." Brown-skinned and clear-eyed, she stared at him. "Why should he be there?—there of all places?"

"Because it's probably where I'd have made for myself if I were in his shoes." There could be no explanations now. "Whether I can get him to come home is another matter."

CHAPTER THREE

1

At two thirty-five in the morning the airport at Klagenfurt had the emptiness and lassitude of a half-abandoned film set. Most of the Viscount's passengers clambered aboard the waiting bus and were driven away. Richard, along with a handful of others, made for the taxi stand and was immediately lucky.

"Steyrhofen?" the driver yawned.

"Correct."

"The only Steyrhofen I know is almost forty kilometers north of here."

"That's it."

"I will have to ask a special price."

"All right, but you'll have to accept sterling. Pounds."

"Not dollars?"

"Not dollars."

Richard was in no mood to haggle. Wearily he tossed his grip onto the rear seat, then ducked in after it. " 'If I were in his shoes,' " Jessica had pressed him. "What's that supposed to mean?" He'd backpedaled on that one, but nothing else. It was a gamble, and he knew it. "I think you're out of your mind." Jessica hadn't minced her words. "I've never heard of anything so harebrained and irresponsible." He'd escaped the house as soon as he could. "What would you rather I did—nothing?"

There was no rain here; the sky was clear and the stars were bright and hard. They left the terminal building and drove through the darkened no-man's-land of the airport to the sodium-lit ring road which led to the city.

"Are you familiar with Steyrhofen?" the driver asked.

"I was there once, years ago."

"At the Rosengarten?"

"Is that the hotel?"

"The only one."

"That's where we were, then—the Rosengarten."

We, he'd said. He leaned back, limp and leaden-eyed, and wondered once more what the chances were. Neon blinked ahead and he translated the slogan that sold a make of Swiss watch: TIME DISCLOSES ALL. They filtered north from the fast highway after only a few minutes, before even reaching the outskirts of Klagenfurt, a stream and a railway track keeping the side road company. Firs blotched the hills to either side and chalets dotted the empty lower slopes.

"This is the Sonnen valley," the driver intoned like a guide, but Richard wasn't paying attention. Nothing looked the same without the snow. Beneath drooping lids he watched the valley gradually narrow. The railway vanished and the road climbed steadily, crossing and recrossing the stream. A couple of villages briefly hemmed them in, silent and shadowy under the star-scatter. STEYRHOFEN: 21 kms. . . . The vastness of Europe didn't bear thinking about. There was nowhere else to look for Howard and expect to find him. Expect? Yes, he thought subbornly; why not? In Tibbie's bedroom a few hours ago Steyrhofen had seemed an inspiration: now a voice of his own was trying to tell him it was wrong to have deserted her, and he answered it back.

"Were you here before in summer or winter?" the driver wanted to know, easing his boredom.

"Winter."

"Good skiing, eh?"

"Yes, it was good."

A memory or two uncoiled. The road corkscrewed deeper into the valley. Richard's mind was in conflict, a dozen thoughts competing for priority. Mountains reared to left and right and he swallowed to accelerate the effect of the gradual change of altitude. Another ten or fifteen minutes passed, nothing on the road in either direction and glimpses of the stream still tumbling through rock and forest.

"Steyrhofen."

They were into it suddenly, everything compact, much as he remembered it—the outlying houses first and then the cafés and bars and shops patterned around the small central square, across which the church and the Rosengarten faced each other. The taxi whimpered softly to a halt outside the hotel and Richard settled with the driver and got out.

Hope had brought him here, hope and despair and impulsiveness, and it was no time to remind himself how familiar and futile a combination these had been in the past. The driver's final glance was directed at Richard's empty sleeve; he mustn't have noticed it before. You were never skiing with *that,* it implied. "Good night, please," he said in home-made English and drove off, thud-and-whine through the gears. Richard pressed the bell at the side of the hotel's heavy door, vividly aware in the self-same instant of two girls and Howard and himself once ringing it in turn, laughing as they waited, their breath frosting on the air. A close-up flitted in and out of his mind. Disaster had belonged to the future then.

He pressed the bell again, restless and impatient, gazing at the carved wooden balconies and decorated eaves. Not a cat moved in the square, nothing. Three thirty. . . . It seemed as useless to be there as it was unreal. Then he heard the lock being turned. The door was opened cautiously by a short, pasty-faced man in pajamas and dressing gown, who muttered something about there not being a night porter during the summer season.

"You want a room, I suppose?" Priest or no priest, he wasn't pleased.

"Thank you."

"It's almost dawn," the man grumbled.

"I'm sorry."

Richard crossed to the desk. A couple of lights had been switched on and he saw the archway through to the dining room and the steps which led to the cellar bar where the dancing always was. It was people the years changed, places that reminded them of what they once were. The man shuffled around behind the desk and selected a key. "Register later," he said. "I can't be bothered now."

"Have you an Englishman staying here?"

"Several, I expect."

Richard hesitated; Howard would hardly be using his own name. Even so he said: "Someone called Lawrence?"

"I work in the kitchen," the man complained. "Things like that are not my concern." He relinquished the key. "Room 18. First floor, on the right."

Richard turned away and walked up. The cable-car structure was visible from the window of his room: it was claimed that, from the top, one could see beyond three frontiers. The thought started him once more on making out a case for his being there, but it was too late to tread old ground and he broke off. Howard was either in Steyrhofen or he wasn't, and if he was he'd be in the Rosengarten. A few hours would settle it, one way or the other.

He undressed, frustration and uncertainty at war with his fatigue. "Howard. . . . Is that you, Howard?"—Tibbie whispered at him still. Lying with his head on the pillows, he stared sleeplessly both at the dark and the slow gray incoming tide that followed it, remembering a riotous and carefree innocence long since lost.

Finally he slept, though not for more than a couple of hours and never far under. It was almost eight when he woke. Hurriedly he washed and shaved and dressed and went downstairs. A few people were already in the dining room, but Howard wasn't among them; a single glance sufficed. It was early yet, he told himself: these were walkers, climbers. Stupid to be so disappointed. He

189

turned away with the intention of checking at the desk. The name was a stumbling block, but they might notice a facial resemblance just as, given the opportunity, he would recognize Howard's handwriting. He had to sign in, anyhow.

"Breakfast, father?"

"Er . . . presently."

"You can have breakfast here or on the terrace."

He'd forgotten the terrace; in winter it was never used. He followed the waiter's directions and stepped out into the warm morning sunlight to join his own shadow and to find tables set in a walled area of rose-covered trellis. Five or six were occupied; he looked eagerly from one to another. And as if in obedience to the demands of his will, he saw that Howard was there.

2

His throat seemed to constrict. He brushed past another waiter. "Howard," he cried in his excitement, not thinking, the gamble justified, everything miraculously narrowed down to a single moment of discovery. "Howard. . . ." He halted, stock-still.

A shiver passed through the muscles of Howard's face. Coffee spilled from the lifted cup as the shock ran down his arm. Otherwise he sat transfixed, frozen as if in a flashlight snapshot. Seconds passed. "Jesus," he said, teeth clenched, then closed his eyes. Suddenly there was sweat in the creases across his forehead. The cup rattled against the saucer. In a low, urgent voice he said: "Are you alone?"

"Of course."

"Sit down." His eyes darted from table to table: he had survived so much. "Pull out the chair and sit down." Any hint of affability was for the eavesdropper. Life seemed to reenter his limbs and he leaned across the table. "How did you know?"

"I guessed."

"Balls."

"I guessed," Richard said. "Take it or leave it. You gave me a clue yourself. Long shots don't always fail."

Howard fumbled a cigarette into his mouth, all nerves as the reaction hit him. He was more drawn than a week ago. "What clue? When?"

"You spoke about Steyrhofen the day I came home— in the garden at Wyndhams."

"You call that a clue?"

"In the circumstances."

"Who else thought so?"

"Nobody. But I told Jessica. She imagines you're on leave."

Smoke swirled. "You wouldn't lie to me, would you?"

"Not about this."

Howard scowled, suspicion in every glance, in every jerky little move he made. "Why Jessica?"

"She's with Tibbie."

"So?"

"Tibbie's dying, Howard." How unreal the word seemed in the bright sunshine. A girl laughed at another table. "She's asking for you."

"You came to tell me that?"

"It's enough, surely?"

"Enough for what?"

"To weigh with you."

He took his time. "You can't seriously—"

"Oh yes." A waiter moved in, shifting a cup here, a knife there. Richard gave his room number and ordered tea with lemon. "Why not?"

Howard snorted. "You need your head examined."

"Perhaps. But it doesn't alter the facts."

"You know my situation."

"And hers." Richard gestured. "The door of her room doesn't open or shut without her asking if it's you. It's you all the time. No one else. And she hasn't got long. . . . She wants you, Howard."

"It's late in the day for that."

"Not too late."

"You don't know what you're saying." He looked at Richard as though he were an enemy who threatened to undermine his safety by means of weapons he considered obsolete. "How can I possibly go back?"

"The way you came."

He shook his head. "Not on your life."

"You could be in and out in a matter of hours."

"No."

"Today."

"No."

"She may not last until tomorrow."

"No, I said." Howard stubbed the cigarette out furiously. "No."

"Listen—"

"Drop it, will you?"

"Listen," Richard said coldly. "When you needed me a week ago I didn't turn you down. I don't know a hundredth part of what you've done and what you really are and I doubt if I ever will. But, dear God, I pitied you that night. . . . Is everyone expendable but you?" He glared. "This mess you're in—"

"Don't preach."

"You're always saying that." The waiter brought the covered glass of tea and he paused until he'd gone. "I'm not talking about murder. I'm talking about betrayal. That night at Evensham you talked about it too. You spoke about it in terms of allegiance to people and of personal shame. 'There are worse things than betraying your country,' you said—remember? Was it all hogwash? Or have you forgotten the meaning of words? Is it the price of survival that you cheat as you go along and don't feel what others feel any more?" Angrily he knocked a cigarette from Howard's pack. "Tibbie wants to see you before she dies."

"You speak as if—"

"Don't tell me you're going to pitch her on the heap with everyone else." He thought of the heartbreak in the quavering voice all those hundreds of miles away. "Give me a light," he said. The cigarette shook between his lips and he had to steady it. "How did you come? By air?" he prompted.

Howard nodded, but he said: "It's no good. I'd never get away with it."

"The office believes you're sick."

"That doesn't mean a thing. Starey was playing along with Garner weeks ago."

"How close had Garner got to you?"

"Close enough." A chair screeched and he stiffened involuntarily.

"There's been no hue and cry."

"Perhaps not in the press."

"Perhaps not at all. I'm suggesting you moved too soon." Lost your nerve, he almost said.

"I don't think so.

"But you don't *know*, do you?" Richard paused. "Nothing's ever certain for you, is it? Ever. You'd be with your friends if it were instead of hanging about here." With studied cruelty he said: "Don't they appreciate loyalty? Or aren't they interested in small fry? I always thought home was where they took you in, come what may."

"Bastard."

A jug crashed to the floor as Howard pushed to his feet and stormed off. Richard followed, oblivious of the stares. He caught up with Howard outside the main door, in the square.

"I'm sorry."

"Herr Elliott." The waiter had followed them both. "Herr Elliott . . . Your lighter and cigarettes."

"Danke."

The waiter returned inside. "I'm sorry," Richard repeated, and Howard shrugged. They walked together, the silence prickling. In winter the horse-drawn sleighs were hired from here: they had driven with lanterns through the woods, the girls and him and Howard, warm under the rugs, swigging slivovitz from a flask. Now the shops were beginning to open.

"There's a flight around four from Klagenfurt."

No reaction.

"We could be at Wyndhams by eight, and you could be back in Steyrhofen—"

"Don't you ever give up?"

"Not if I can help it."

"It won't work, Richard."

"It must. It's got to." Pity stirred in him again, the terrible promiscuous emotion that always destroyed his sense of responsibility. "You've got one death on your

193

conscience. Don't willfully add another. She wants you, Howard. Needs you."

"In delirium."

"No."

They walked slowly past the church. The dead were here too, like everywhere else, their chances lost or taken.

"Do something for someone else," Richard urged. "Who's on the lookout for a nonexistent Mr. Elliott?"

Richard glanced at him searchingly, but in profile the face yielded nothing. The curling rink where the four of them had won a novices' challenge competition was off to their right.

"She wasn't delirious when I left. She was choosing what she asked for and all the time it was you." He stopped abruptly, checking Howard by the arm. "Say yes, for God's sake."

"What guarantees can you give?"

"None," he snapped with impatience and regret. "I don't work your way."

"Why should I adopt yours?"

"For Tibbie's sake. And because you're in a void and there aren't any options open and you're as uncertain of the future as you're imprisoned by the past. But most of all for Tibbie's sake."

"When did she ever want us?"

"Now," Richard said, as he'd said once before. "I'm only talking of now."

"I've had 'nows' myself."

"Come on home."

"You've had them as well. You've needed her in your day. Her . . . him. Someone."

"Perhaps."

"Perhaps nothing. Everything else was a substitute."

"We weren't dying," Richard persevered.

"Sometimes it felt like it."

"Say good-bye to her, Howard. Don't betray her too."

3

He knew about then that he would win. But it still took time—an hour, at least an hour and maybe more:

he didn't measure it or experience any sense of triumph when Howard finally conceded. They were on a hillside track above the village. They walked back in silence, uneasy with each other, almost hostile; it was strange. Richard signed in at the Rosengarten and, simultaneously, asked for his bill. The clerk was amused. "Are you leaving too, Herr Elliott?"

"Not yet awhile. You'll see me around tomorrow as usual."

The taxis were near the cable-car station. They drank first—brandy—needing it, both of them, but for different reasons. Just after eleven they started down the Sonnen valley in a Volkswagen. Earlier, when Howard's resistance was beginning to wilt, he'd argued feebly that they'd never get on a plane that day. Now he was making conditions. "What time's the Lufthansa night flight out of London?"

"Ten minutes after midnight."

"I want a firm reservation as a first priority."

"There won't be any problem about that. We were half empty."

"Even so."

He was tense already, and the tension was contagious. Richard felt it too. A tactical success had made him an accomplice, a fellow conspirator. There was no elation. Howard would have five hours or so between touchdown and takeoff, perhaps three to quench Tibbie's thirst for him. "Would you have preferred indifference from her?" Richard had argued doggedly. "Is life so meaningless that it's of no consequence whether she needs you or not?" Love was a word he had not dared to use. Love, affection, loyalty, pity—were they all one, or was it a descending scale?

The valley widened and the road reached stream-level. The railway reappeared, curving in from behind the woods. They met the main highway and headed for the airport, keeping to the center lane. It was exactly noon when they entered the terminal building.

"Here." Howard produced some American money. "You do it. . . . Bruce Elliott. You'd better take the passport —just in case."

"Where will I find you?"

"In the bar."

Richard joined him there a quarter of an hour later. Howard hadn't removed his dark glasses and he had somehow contrived a distance between himself and his nearest neighbor. "No trouble?"

"None at all."

Richard returned his passport and gave him the tickets to examine. He did so critically, as if they were captured documents. He was nervy now, his control less impeccable—or was that imagination? Richard reflected on the subtle falsehood of the passport photograph: but for knowing he would never have doubted its likeness. To whom, though? Howard was layer upon layer. Even the façade seemed different, more contrived, when one was an ally.

Howard drained his glass and signaled for more. He was a long way from danger, but he couldn't relax.

"Take it easy," Richard warned at the third scotch.

"All right, all right."

They kept themselves to themselves when they lunched in the restaurant. There was nothing to talk about. All the talking was done, the forbidden ground agreed upon. "Look," Howard had stipulated. "I'll come, but leave the past alone. No questions—is that understood?"

Outside, the runways simmered in a burst of afternoon heat. They booked in shortly before the flight was announced and moved to the departure lounge. Howard was sweating a little. Only a handful of people waited with them—fifteen, perhaps twenty. After a few minutes a blond ground stewardess came through the barrier. Incredibly she said: "Mr. Elliott?" She glanced from side to side. "Mr. Bruce Elliott?"

Howard stiffened. "What is it?" First time he couldn't get it out.

"We are making a check." The fixed smile was polite and professional. "You have no luggage, is that correct? None at all?"

"Correct," he said.

"Thank you, sir."

She swiveled, heel-and-toe, and went quickly away.

Howard's nerves were suddenly there for all to see. He mopped his face. The granite inner discipline had crumbled since Macerda; fear would always be quicker, stronger. It had brutalized him once, mauled and maimed him. Alarm flecked his eyes, inseparable from terror and the remembered escalation into nightmare.

"It's okay," Richard said urgently. "Everything's okay."

They all went like sheep down the incline with their boarding cards and crossed the apron to the aircraft. The takeoff preliminaries were minimal. The sun streamed and the engines whined in pre-ignition protest. One-handed, Richard clipped his seat belt. Goddard and Escobar, Sharkey and Uziama—the memories were inescapable, but they were not for now. Tibbie was enough for now, Tibbie and the full extent of what he'd asked of Howard.

4

Touchdown was a double jolt and the reverse thrust's roar. They trundled toward the dispersal bay, ears singing as the aircraft wheeled and parked and the engines died. Dusk was on its way, the sky a pink and purple smear. People were getting to their feet, struggling into coats, collecting hand luggage, but neither Howard nor Richard moved until the steps were in position.

"Go first," Howard said. "And keep away from me."

Richard nodded: one Lawrence on the passenger list was a Lawrence too many. Common sense told him that it was stupid to expect that separation might somehow be a safeguard, but it wasn't an occasion for common sense. He was jittery, and not for himself. He followed a young couple through the door. "No rain?" The girl postured like a comic. "Can this be England?" Their casualness was enviable: a hidden bottle of scent, perhaps, or some surplus cognac—what had they to fear? Richard mounted the glass-walled ramp and took his place near the front of the line for immigration. The thought of Garner loomed. Two men were at the desk, one standing; he looked over his colleague's shoulder as Richard's passport was studied. Was it its newness that made them curious? "Thank you, padre," the seated man said impassively, and Richard's heart thumped. A tick was placed against his name on the typed list at the official's elbow.

He went about halfway in the direction of customs, then found himself unable to go any further without looking back. Howard was two from the desk. Richard watched the queue shuffle forward. Howard's face had the stiffness of a mask. He was next in line now, make or break only seconds away. Richard held his breath. How small the risks had seemed in Steyrhofen—to him. Howard took one more step and handed the passport across—Elliott, Bruce Elliott, company director. Color of eyes, color of hair. . . . Time had slowed its pace. One of the men said something—his lips moved and he looked up. Howard leaned forward. "Yes," he seemed to be answering. The pages were thumbed back and forth. . . . Place of birth, date of birth. . . . Suddenly the passport was snapped to and Howard's hand went out. Richard felt himself released. With an intensity of feeling he turned and went in search of his grip.

For the time being it was over; Howard was clear, and it didn't bear thinking about that he'd have to run the gauntlet again in a few hours.

"Nothing to declare—no."

Richard made his way to the concourse, uncertain where to wait. Presently Howard walked by. He glanced at Richard almost without recognition and Richard followed him to where the taxis were.

"Marsden."

They got in. Howard showed the strain. The tension hadn't left him. His eyes had a raw, staring look.

"What did he say?"

"Who?"

"At immigration."

"He pointed out that I'll need to renew the passport in a month."

In a film it might have released some vicarious laughter. But not from them; not in real life. The dark was closing in. Richard had a sudden desire to say: "You won't regret this when Tibbie sees you"—but he could not. Anything he said would be inadequate, superfluous, an intrusion.

198

"Whereabouts in Marsden, sir?"

"A place called Wyndhams. I'll direct you when we reach the village."

Jessica's Mini was still in the drive, off to one side by the garage. There were lights in nearly every window, giving the house a mellow softness it didn't deserve. Richard rang and they waited, the two of them, silence gradually taking hold as the car receded.

Inside, someone fumbled for the catch. There was a click, and the door opened. Mrs. Wood peered at them a trifle vaguely, slow to respond, stairs and an empty hall behind her.

"Hallo, Mrs. Wood. . . . How is she?"

"Mr. Howard!"

"How *is* she?"

It was Richard who spoke, but she looked at Howard as if only he were there. With a hand nervously to her throat she said: "She's dead, Mr. Howard."

"No. . . ."

"This morning." There was apprehension in her voice as well as tears. "She died this morning."

"No." Like a punctuation mark. "No."

"Howard?"

Jessica was on the stairs, pale and incredulous. A tall slim man emerged from the study, balding, stern-faced; he might have been a solicitor. Another man, shorter, followed him. They came eagerly, sure of themselves.

"Commander Lawrence? Howard Lawrence?"

"Yes."

Everything was happening at once. "I am Detective Superintendent James Wright of the Metropolitan Police, Special Branch, and I have with me a warrant for your arrest—"

Howard swung fiercely on Richard. "Liar!" He spat it out, at bay. "You lied to me."

"No!"

"You gave your word."

"And kept it. . . . I swear."

"They were waiting for me and you knew it."

Anguished, Richard could not speak. All his life he was

199

to remember a moment of absolute stillness and the sound of sobbing about his ears.

CHAPTER FOUR

1

They buried Tibbie at Marsden. John Wyatt sang the Requiem in an almost empty church, invoking the everlasting mercy in the presence of the day nurse and Taplow and Mrs. Wood. Jessica stayed away, and Richard didn't blame her; the press had badgered for days. They lurked in the vicinity as indiscreetly as they dared, but it was doubtful whether it was worth their while. Howard came and went in a police car which backed right up to the porch to deliver him and moved around to the vestry door to collect. In between he sat in the rear pew during mass and stood at the graveside for the final prayers, flanked by two anonymous companions.

The flowers and wreaths seemed indecently beautiful in the dull September light. When John Wyatt spattered the coffin with water and scooped earth into the pit, it fell with a hollow sound, as if the immaculate box were empty and Tibbie had never been. It was awful to hear, just as it was awful for Richard to face Howard across the grave and to be stonily refused so much as a glance. He was resigned to death, but not to life, not as it was. NAVAL OFFICER ARRESTED, the headlines had shouted. NIGHT DRAMA AT SURREY HOUSE.

John Wyatt closed his missal; it was over. Dust to dust. . . . The little group seemed reluctant to disperse. Howard was the first to leave, accompanied, stride for stride. For a moment Richard remained quite still; time had run out, but his desperation couldn't accept it and he suddenly rounded the grave and went after him. Ten paces from the car he stopped.

"D'you think I'd help to trap my own brother?"

They had opened the rear door and were waiting for Howard to get in.

"Do you?"

Howard turned, and his gaze was long and lasting. With pitiless calm he said: "There's more to it than that."

A shadow heaved in Richard's mind. "More to what?"

And in a clear voice that reverberated with a ringing tone off the flint-stone walls of the church, Howard replied: "I've written to you."

You asked me a question in Steyrhofen, part of the letter read. *One of the many you hooked me with. Is everyone expendable except you?—that's what you said. So now I've got a question of my own. And it's this: is everyone expendable on your behalf? Ask yourself that. Go back to the time you quit the Air Force and ask yourself that—from Rosalind on. What price do others have to pay for your good intentions? . . .*

"That's hard," Daniel Somerset remarked. "He's bitter, of course. It's understandable, everything taken into account. Even so, that's hard."

"He thinks I failed him."

"Did you?"

"Not in the way he means."

"In what way, then?"

With a despairing gesture, Richard said: "I'm not sure."

In my opinion we're neither of us what we thought we were. I'm making no comparison, but you've had your victims too. . . .

"Did he have victims?" Daniel Somerset asked mercilessly.

"I've no idea."

"It's a sad letter. What he says here, for instance—*Have you wept tears for Tibbie? Not to my knowledge. Yet you expected me to put myself at risk on her behalf. Or was it yours? All the evidence indicates that pity is no more to you than something you employ to make demands on others. . . .*

201

Richard interrupted: "If he had gone where he intended going they would have failed him as well."

"You seem very certain."

"He wouldn't have hesitated otherwise. It wasn't an ideological thing with him. There would have been times when he must have told himself it was, but it was really a search of quite another kind."

"We all have a blind side."

"He once mentioned respect and appreciation, but these were only stand-ins for what he was really after."

"And what was that?"

Richard shrugged. "Love?" he suggested. "There was a lack of it at Wyndhams. One always desires what one never had—if not for oneself then as an offering to others."

"No matter what the cost?"

Richard swallowed. He thought of Howard and the grudge he so often seemed to bear. Remorse struggled in him as he reflected on how it must have been—the constant searching and the endless new beginnings, the uncertain moments of contentment and the awful periods of desolation, the women and the risks and the terrible lack of trust and the murdered Portuguese who now would follow him everywhere.

"We are taught," Daniel Somerset was saying, "to hate the sin and love the sinner."

Richard moved impatiently; he expected more than clichés.

"We are also taught to look critically at ourselves. It's a hard letter, I grant you. Fierce. But remember this about your brother: when he chose to return with you it was a totally unselfish act. And that's love, surely? The only casualty could have been himself, and he knew it."

Richard reached for the letter. "You're saying that he's right, aren't you? . . . About me."

The older priest paused, restrained in what he was about to answer by the awareness of the stump in the pinned-up sleeve. "All I'm saying, Richard, is that I shouldn't have thought—after what I've read—that he was ever likely to have confused what he did with duty."